GATOR ROLL

G.W. Reynolds III

ISBN 978-1934666-64-7

Cover Design by Summer Morris

Published and distributed by:
High-Pitched Hum Publishing
321 15th Street North
Jacksonville Beach, Florida 32250

Contact High-Pitched Hum Publishing at
www.highpitchedhum.net

This is a work of fiction. The literary perceptions and insights are based on the author's experience. All names and places not historical, characters and incidents are either products of the author's imagination or are used fictitiously.

High-Pitched Hum
Publishing

GATOR ROLL

G.W. Reynolds III

PRELUDE

The shrimper's village of Mayport, Florida had been quiet during the week after the dead and disfigured bodies were found and removed from under the grape arbor below the sand hill and the oak tree. The authorities knew it had to have been a number of Mayport citizens who committed the merciless slaughter of the four drifters. They also knew the other dead body found in the ditch on the Fort George side of the St. Johns River was connected to the four bodies killed in Mayport. As usual, no one in Mayport seemed to know anything about the brutal killings. The investigation was at a standstill and without officers David Boos and Paul Short there to question the right people, the investigation would move slowly and end in that first week. The fact that the bodies had no identification on them and they were not recognizable made it even more difficult to continue with any type of investigation. It ended almost before it got started.

Jason, Billy and Rebecca Coolie made it to the Giant's Motel in Gibsonton, Florida. They stayed at the ultimate black honky tonk, Porter's Night Moves, a little longer than they had expected. Being with Nadine Porter and Rebecca Coolie another night was more than worth it for Jason. The two women's sexual activity together was so intense that Jason felt they liked each other more than they liked him. He was sure they would be just as happy without him in the bed with them. That excited him even more.

Officers David Boos and Paul Short also made their way to Ruskin, Florida just a few miles south of the Giant's Motel. They stopped there and questioned the Giant, Big Bob, but they were staying in a motel on Bahia Beach just south of the Giant's Motel. They also knew Big Bob would not give them any information about Tom Green, but they questioned him anyway, just in case he might give them something to work with. He did not do so. Officers Boos and Short were on a mission to bring Tom Green back to Mayport to pay for his crimes from the past. Money had its hold on the two lawmen.

Mr. King was torn and confused about Anna Hamilton's quick and unexpected appearance back into his life and her just as quick and unexpected exit. His mind was in a fog of disappointment and lack of understanding. He didn't want to think about it but he had to entertain the possibility that the carousel had caused the strange dreams and Anna Hamilton was never really there with him. He shook those thoughts from his head and remembered the sex he had with the self-proclaimed witch. He knew that was real. It had to be. At times he could smell her in his room.

Miss Margaret's house had been quiet and sad, too. The atmosphere changed drastically from the moment she and her four daughters returned home from participating in the awful carnage under the grape arbor. Nothing and no one in that house would ever be the same. The store was open that week, but Miss Margaret was the only one who worked. She got up every morning, opened the store and stayed until she got tired and decided to go home, closing at all different hours, only to return the next morning. She did spend one full night in the store and opened the next morning wearing the same clothes she had worn the day before. She did not ask her daughters to help her and they did not offer to do so. Miss Margaret was different. They were all different.

Two of her daughters, Susan and Peggy, left together early that morning after Miss Margaret went to the store. They were hoping to be able to stay with their Aunt Peggy and her live-in friend and lover, Betty. Aunt Peggy and Betty had doubled teamed men in their bed from time to time, but Betty preferred the one on one with her roommate. Aunt Peggy liked sex no matter how it came her way. Her free spirited attitude captivated her younger relatives. Aunt Peggy was always talking about life and relationships. The girls had learned a great deal from their Aunt Peggy.

Sofia remained at the house, locked in her bedroom most of the week. During that time Miss Margaret heard Sofia moving around in her room but did not speak to her youngest child. Miss Margaret had seen Margie the day after the killings but they did not speak either. Margie left later that week when her mother was at the store. No one saw her leave. Miss Margaret's beautiful family was shattered into pieces with little chance of mending or redemption.

Mary C. sat on the front porch drinking her morning coffee with Mr. John King. They both had talked to the police but had no information to give. The police said the two drifters Mary C. killed outside the house were both extremely dangerous fugitives wanted by the law for murder and rape. It seemed Mary C. had done the town and the police a great service by killing them both. Her philosophy of "shoot first and find out who they are later" was in full force and reasonable at the time.

Mr. John King had visited the crime scene at the grape arbor and knew five of Mayport's finest females were the culprits of the bloody aftermath. It would be another secret he would burn deep into his belly, as he had done many times before. They were all learning the true art of burning secrets in your belly. His thoughts were of his time with Anna Hamilton and he wondered where she was, now. Was she truly from the underworld of dreams? Was she the witch she had always proclaimed to be? Or was she just another one of the insane who fell into people's lives now and then? Mr. King was a three question man. He was amazed at his relationships and secrets with women like Mary C., Ana Kara, Anna Hamilton and now Miss Margaret and her four daughters. His haunted house, the magic carousel, the dreams of Purgatory and the mass killings had him wanting to run away for the first time in his life. It was all too much for one man, even a man with few fears.

CHAPTER ONE

Mary C. sipped her coffee and looked out at the river. She looked at Mr. King sitting next to her and knew when he was in deep thought, so she went deep as well. It was not a morning for talk. Mary C. thought about her conversation and day in church with Miss Carolyn. Was there true forgiveness for all she had done in her life of blood, evil and mortal sins? Mary C. shook her head and smiled at the ridiculous thought of her redemption. She wondered why she would harbor such a foolish notion. She didn't know why it seemed so possible when Miss Carolyn spoke the words of encouragement. In Mary C.'s mind, Miss Carolyn had a gift. Before she would try to fix her life, Mary C. knew she had to get Jason and Billy back to Mayport for her own piece of mind. It was strange that no one was thinking about Miss Stark's diamond and ruby necklace. They had it and that was all that mattered for now.

The ferry horn sounded as the big car carrier left the Fort George side of the river, interrupting the two deep thinkers. It was as if it was time to return to the reality of the porch. A new red truck rolled up to the front of the haunted house. They both looked up as Miss Carolyn rolled the window down on the passenger's side of her new truck. Mary C. leaned forward in her rocking chair when she recognized the new truck and Miss Carolyn at the window. There was a man driving Miss Carolyn's new truck. Mary C. had not seen Miss Carolyn with a man in quite some time. Mr. King looked into the truck and recognized Miss Carolyn's husband, George. He was one of the Mayport shrimpers who were always gone. He was either shrimping off the coast of Texas, down in Fort Myers, the Dry Tortugas, or South America; anywhere, but Mayport. Mary C. could see the joyous look on Miss Carolyn's angel face.

"Mornin' Mary C...John."

Mary C. smiled and John lifted his coffee cup as a salute and good morning greeting. Their voices were in stereo. "Mornin' Miss Carolyn." Mary C. nodded her head toward the driver. Miss Carolyn was still smiling.

"George just got back last night. He was gone six months this time. He's droppin' me off at the restaurant, I got the long day, today. I'd like to take the day off but I made a commitment to Mr. Strickland." Miss Carolyn smiled at Mary C. and directed her question to Mr. King. "Have you seen my new truck?"

Mr. King raised his cup again. "I heard about it. It's a pretty thing." He looked into the truck. "Welcome home, George. It's good to see you safe and sound."

"Good to be home, John. It's always good to be home." George looked at Mary C. "Some gift." He touched Miss Carolyn's shoulder. "She's a happy woman."

Miss Carolyn was excited as she smiled at Mary C. "I wanted to come by and tell you they are really working on your house out there. They got it framed in and looks like they'll be closin' her up and dryin' her in before the weeks done. We're gonna be neighbors soon. I'm very excited about all this. And my truck is wonderful."

Mary C. did love Miss Carolyn. She smiled and nodded. She did not like George sitting in the driver's seat, but she did respond to Miss Carolyn.

"I gotta get out there and see what's goin' on. I've been a little pre-occupied around here, lately." Mary C. had a mind flash of her pulling the trigger of a shotgun, but shook the vision from her head. "I'll try to make it out there today if I can."

Miss Carolyn's face took on a serious look. "I heard about those people bein' killed near the oak tree. What a terrible thing to happen so close to home." She shook her head and directed her thoughts to Mary C. "And you had to defend yourself against those awful two men right here on this porch. You have always been so brave. Thank God we didn't lose you. Mayport sure has her fill of people dyin', don't she?"

Mr. King nodded his head in agreement, as Miss Carolyn changed her facial expression and smiled her usual "God bless you" smile. "Well, I shouldn't have talked about sad things on such a wonderful day. It was great seein' you two this mornin'. I gotta go get set up for the lunch crowd. Y'all have a good day."

The red truck moved away from the house. John King's voice sounded very strange to Mary C. "That's one bad man, right there. How he ever won Carolyn's heart will always be a mystery to me. All of us for that matter."

Mary C. was taken aback by Mr. King's comment. "Are you talkin' about, George?" Mr. King nodded but he did not speak. Mary C. went on. "I don't know much about him. I don't like him, though. What do you mean, 'He's one bad man'?"

"Mean, tough, bad, you know. He's from way up North. Damn Yankee came here with the Navy, found Carolyn workin' over at the Fish Bowl in East Mayport, and he decided to stay here. He came in mean and got even meaner the longer he stayed."

Mary C. was puzzled and intrigued by Mr. King's words. "Why do you say he got meaner?"

Mr. King had the answer. "He couldn't help it. It was the way it just happened. He had no way out. It was either get meaner or die."

Even with Mary C.'s primary thoughts of getting Jason

and Billy back from their self-induced exile at the Giant's Motel in Gibsonton, Florida, Mr. King's words about George had Mary C.'s attention.

"John, tell me about Miss Carolyn and George."

Mr. King did not respond to her request. He turned his head away from her and his attention fell on the two young boys walking past his porch. Mr. King stared at the two boys for a second as if he was watching them with caution. Mary C. turned to look in the same direction, as the Croom twins walked by. Both boys were carrying a cane pole and a small bait bag. They stared and didn't talk at first. Mary C. never liked the strange young boys. A chill ran through Mr. King's body. He was compelled to speak to the identical twins.

"Mornin' boys. Y'all goin' fishin'?"

Chuck had the answer. "No. We're gonna shove these cane pole up our butt holes."

The insane boys both laughed at their nasty poetic answer then moved away from the porch. Mr. King was not expecting such an odd and disrespectful response to his innocent question. Mary C. was the first to respond.

"You can't be nice to those two, John. There's somethin' bad wrong with those boys. They are the nastiest young boys to ever grow up here in Mayport. Now, don't get me wrong. There's been some bad children around here before, but those two are more than just bad boys. These two have something evil growing inside 'em and the older they get the bigger it gets."

Mr. King squinted his eyes. "Damn, Mary C., I had a strange feeling when they walked up and now I got the willies listening to you. I thought with all the things that happened to them two, maybe they was just messed up and would heal with time. They lost their mama and big brother and that daddy of theirs is a poor excuse for a man. They got nobody to turn to, just each other."

Mary C. had no sympathy, at all, for the sadness the twins had endured. "Those things have nothing to do with the evil inside those two. It's been festerin' from the moment the air touched 'em."

"Holy Moly, Mary C., I don't want to think about devil children walking around here. We've had enough evil and meanness in the last few years to last a hundred lifetimes, don't ya think?"

Mary C. knew Mr. King was referring to a number of her moments of revenge and the use of her shotgun. "John, like I've said before, I know things. I know those boys are on this earth to do hateful things. I'm afraid for the ones who get in their way or just cross their paths."

Mr. King wanted no more of the scary conversation. "Okay, I'm done with creepy talk. Why don't we ride out and see how your house is lookin'?"

Mary C. had a better idea. "Why don't we pack a few clothes and take a ride to the Giant's Motel and maybe you will see Ana Kara again? We can stop by my new house on the way out."

John smiled. He wanted to get away. "Damn, Mary C., you do have a good idea there. Let's do it. Let's get away from here."

They both turned to walk into the house but stopped when they heard laughter to the right of the porch. Mary C. turned first and then Mr. King. For some reason, goose-bumps filled their arms when they saw the twins had returned and they were looking over the porch railing. The boys were only visible from the nose up, with their black eyes the focal point. Chuck spoke first in a strange deep voice that did not fit his age.

"Come she, come." He waited for a response but did not get one. "Come she, come."

Mr. King looked at Mary C. She shook her head, as to say, "don't answer".

They both knew the boy was playing the children's word game, "Come she, come".

The proper response was, "What letter she come bye?"

This was usually followed by the hint of the first letter in the word you were searching for. Mary C. was concerned and cautious and did not want to play any game with the insane twins. The two adults stared at the four eyes looking over the railing. Chuck tried one more time.

"Come she, come." He looked at his twin brother. "Come she, come."

Buck realized the two adults were not going to play. He knew what to say. "What letter she come by?"

Chuck was ready and quick with his single letter hint, "T".

Both boys pulled themselves up and stood on the outside edge of the porch holding on to the top of the railing. At the exact same time, as if they had rehearsed it over and over again, they both yelled "titties" for the "T" word they were looking for. They jumped down from the porch, grabbed their cane poles and ran away again.

Mary C. looked at Mr. King. "Someone needs to put some leather on those lily white butts."

Mr. King nodded his head. "Or perhaps a cane pole, up the butt hole."

They both walked into the house and Mary C. forgot about learning more about Miss Carolyn's husband.

At the ripe old age of thirteen, the Croom twins, Chuck and Buck, were already insane. They were much more than just different. The only word is insane. They were born with tainted blood, filled with mildew. Evil and mayhem exploded in their black eyes. The cute and innocent freckles dotting their cheeks were a contradiction to the darkness in their minds. The boys were hateful and bathed in the discomfort and pain of others, both human and animal.

Their older brother, Pee Wee, was a nervous wreck at age fourteen. His name was a reference to his size and stature. He was a year older, but much smaller than his two younger brothers. Each twin actually doubled him in size. Pee Wee was afraid of his younger brothers. They had hurt him before. He tried to stay away from them whenever he could. He spent his days on guard and concerned for his physical welfare, causing serious damage to his mental health and positive thoughts. It was an awful way for a young boy to live.

The constant reminder of how small he was destroyed any speck of self-esteem or confidence he tried to establish. Pee Wee felt safe when his older brother Joe was alive, but with Joe dying from being attacked by the devil dog, Abaddon, Pee Wee was left alone to deal with his evil siblings. His mother had also died. She was another safety valve that took the pressure of the twins off of Pee Wee's little shoulders. They had taken away his innocence and positive outlook on life.

Some folks said Chuck and Buck became hateful after they saw their brother Joe being filled by the devil dog. It warped their little minds. Perhaps that awful event added to the insanity, but they were pure evil years before that day.

When Mary C., Miss Margaret and the girls killed the drifters under the grape arbor, Chuck and Buck touched the dead bodies and made jokes about the carnage. They even squeezed the breasts of the dead lady. She had no face left, but that did not matter to the boys. She did have big breasts.

They watched Margie during her self satisfying ritual at the tree. They had watched the drifters take turns having sex with the women under the grape arbor. The twins knew far too much about life and death. They created misery of others on a daily basis and they enjoyed every minute of it.

Chuck and Buck stood on the Little Jetty rocks with the lines of their cane poles in the water. They would spend hours fishing and torturing every fish they caught. They never took any of the catch back home to cook and eat. The twins were only interested in watching the fish squirm in pain as they cut their eyes out and threw them back into the water, thinking it was funny that the fish would be blind. The twins had black hearts. It was the mildew in their blood.

Miss Margaret was waiting on a customer at the store. It

was easy to see she was not her usual happy and friendly self. The customer was Robert Fussell. He was a local man, but did not live in the town of Mayport. Robert worked for the Jacksonville Fire Department and spent a great deal of his off time in Mayport fishing at the Little Jetties, going out on the shrimp boats and fishing for big Red Snapper on the party boat Miss Wilma. Robert loved the water and all that went with it. He loved Mayport. He was in the store buying a few things for a day of fishing at the Little Jetties. He stood at the counter with his items. Robert was a regular customer at the store on his visits to Mayport and he knew Miss Margaret had a distant and strange look about her that particular day. He also noticed that he did not get the traditional greeting all the customers were used to receiving. Miss Margaret had her head down as she tallied his selection. Robert thought perhaps something had happened to a family member. He was not one to pry into the business of others but he was interested and compelled to speak.

"Good morning, Miss Margaret. I hope all is well with you and yours. It's always nice to see you."

Miss Margaret realized she was wearing her sadness like a mask and it was easy to read it on her face. She took a strange deep breath as if she had to force herself to respond. "Good morning to you, too, Robert. I do apologize for my silence this morning."

Robert Fussell smiled. "Can't be feelin' great every day, Miss Margaret. It wouldn't be natural if we didn't have a bad day, now and then." Miss Margaret forced a smile and thought to herself, *If you only knew*.

But he didn't know. However, he did know how to mind his own business. He smiled, paid for his fishing gear and nodded his head as a good-bye. The bell on the front door sounded as he left. Miss Margaret was glad she was alone again.

Margie, Miss Margaret's eldest daughter, walked away from the front desk at the Sand Piper Hotel located on the

Atlantic Ocean in Jacksonville Beach. She had paid to stay for one night and had her room key in her hand. Margie wrote down a false name when she registered. The clerk did not even question her at all. He just took her money and handed her the key. The once high-class and elegant hotel was not what it used to be. It had become a haven for the local ladies of the evening, a place for one night stands and a locker club where drunk sailors could rent a bed and sleep it off and sober up before retuning to the Navy Base.

As Margie walked up the stairs and located her room on the third floor, she passed a brightly dressed woman kissing a uniformed sailor in the corner of the hall. The sailor squeezed one of the woman's breasts as they kissed. She recognized sexual noises she heard coming from the rooms as she walked by. One man wearing only his boxer shorts lay on the hall floor a few feet from the door to her room. She moved quickly when she saw her room number and unlocked the door. The room was dark and she had to find the light. Margie was afraid.

Robert Fussell walked on the rocks of the Little Jetties. He struggled for a few seconds trying to balance himself, as he carried his rod and reel and tackle box over the uneven rocks. He stopped to sit on the first flat top rock he felt was a good spot to spend a few hours of fishing. He had been waiting for this time on the water for the entire week. Robert Fussell loved the water and catching fish.

At first, he did not notice the Croom twins sitting on the rocks a few yards to his left. He was more interested in finding that one comfortable rock to settle on. He sat down and prepared his equipment. As he baited his hook, something hit him on the side of his head. He reached up and realized the hook and lead sinker on one of the twin's cane poles had hit him in the head. Then it moved away. He looked toward the boys.

"Hey boys, be careful. You almost took my ear off. Watch what you're doin' over there."

It was Chuck's line that sailed in Mr. Fussell's direction. "Sorry mister, I didn't see ya, over there. Are ya all right?"

Mr. Fussell was not happy with how careless the boy was. "I'm fine, but please be careful. Ain't nothin' worse than a fish hook in the eye."

The twins both made strange faces but did not respond. They went back to fishing. Mr. Fussell did, too.

Mr. King drove his mint condition 1955 Ford up to the front of Mary C.'s newly framed in house. She was in the passenger's seat. They had both packed a few items for the trip to the Giant's Motel. They stepped out of the car and Mary C. talked to one of the carpenters for a few minutes. Mr. King walked around the structure. He looked across through the wooded area between Miss Carolyn's house and Mary C.'s property. He could see her house through the cabbage palms and oak trees. Mary C. looked in that direction when she saw Miss Carolyn's new red truck roll up into the front yard. Mary C. walked up next to Mr. King as George got out of the red truck and walked into the house. Mary C. had to speak her mind.

"I hope he's good to Miss Carolyn. He better take care of that truck."

Mr. King only nodded his head. He knew Mary C. meant what she said. She did love Miss Carolyn. She surprised Mr. King when she changed her mind about the trip to Gibsonton.

"John, will you be very disappointed if we take our trip in a day or so?"

Mr. King knew it was unusual for Mary C. to change her mind, especially when it came to Jason and Billy. He would do whatever she wanted with no questions asked.

"I won't be disappointed at all. We'll go when you want."

Mary C. looked toward Miss Carolyn's house again and stared for a few seconds. Then she turned to continue her inspection of her soon to be framed in Jim Walter Home.

About fifteen minutes of fishing had passed since the mishap with Chuck's cane pole line. Robert Fussell had caught one sheepshead, one drum, and one red. The three river catfish were not on his stringer. He had thrown them back into the water. He was having a fun day on the Little Jetties. Mr. Fussell had paid very little attention to the twins and their evil ritual of torturing the fish they caught. His great day on the Little Jetties was going to come to an end.

When the fishing line hit his face for the second time it was like the end of a bull whip had popped him on his upper lip. It felt like someone had lit a match and held it to his face. He dropped his rod on the rocks and grabbed his mouth with this hand. Mr. Fussell knew right away he had a fishing hook stuck in this upper lip. He held the hook and line in his hand as he turned to see one of the twins holding the cane pole with the line attached. It was Chuck's line again. He tried to pull the line back but Mr. Fussell held it tight and would not let the boy pull it away.

"Stop! Please stop! The hook is in my mouth! Stop pulling the line! Please stop!"

Chuck gave the line one more pull as if he did not hear the man's plea. But, Mr. Fussell was not letting go of his hold on that line.

"I said stop pulling the line! The hook is in my lip! What's wrong with you? Stop, damn it!"

Mr. Fussell realized that Chuck did not drop the cane pole and the young boy could pull the line whenever he wanted. It was unsettling that the boy had not released his hold on the cane pole as he had requested. Mr. Fussell held on to the line and started making his way toward the boys. He pulled more line to his hand as he got closer. He was shocked that Chuck still had the cane pole in his hand. It was like the boy was waiting on him to relax so he could pull the line again. His lip was bleeding and the blood was running down is chin and neck. He held the fishing line with a death grip. He was not going to let the insane boy pull that line and jerk the hook out of his lip. Mr. Fussell was only a few yards away from the boys when he stopped. He was afraid to get too close to the young boys. Even though they were young, they were big boys. Mr. Fussell thought they could easily take down a man if they worked together. He was in enough pain. He didn't need to be knocked down on the jetty rocks by the two hoodlums. The three stared at one another for only a few seconds. Mr. Fussell had the line wrapped around his hand so Chuck could get no slack and pull the cane pole. Robert Fussell gritted his teeth in pain as he spoke directly to Chuck.

"Now, I ain't too sure why you are still holding that pole when you know your hook is in my lip. I'd hate to think you would like to hurt me even more. I'm gonna ask you one time to please put the pole down so I can get this thing out of my mouth. If you don't, I'll know I have to put it down for you." Even though he was mad and in pain, Mr. Fussell's voice was calm as he addressed the boys. He looked at Buck. "What's your name, boy?"

"Buck."

"Well Buck, while your brother's deciding if he's gonna put the pole down or not, you're gonna go get my tackle box and bring it over here to me."

It was obvious Chuck didn't like it when Buck moved across the rocks toward the tackle box with no hesitation at all. He moved past Mr. Fussell and hurried over the rocks.

Mr. Fussell watched Buck as he worked his way to the tackle box. "Thanks young man." He turned back to Chuck. The young boy was gone but the cane pole was lying on the rocks. When Buck realized Chuck was gone, he dropped the tackle box and climbed over the rocks and away from Mr. Fussell. The tackle box fell between the rocks but did not break or pop open.

Robert Fussell would have to do some maneuvering over the rocks, but at least he did not have to worry about the hook being jerked from his lip. He pulled the cane pole towards him so he could carry it to the location of the tackle box. The box was wedged between two rocks but it was not out of his reach. Once he had the box he was able to get his wire clippers and cut the line that was attached to the hook. Being free from the cane pole was what he needed. He took the cane pole and threw it in the river.

Mr. Fussell knew he would need a mirror and possibly some help to remove the hook from his upper lip. He gathered his fishing gear and made his way over the rocks toward his truck. It never crossed his mind that they could have done anymore damage that day but when he got to his truck it had four flat tires and two broken tail lights. He could not see the Croom twins but he felt they were watching him.

CHAPTER TWO

Mary C. and Mr. King were back at the haunted house. He wasn't sure why Mary C. postponed the trip but he would wait for an explanation if she wanted to share it with him. He had poured himself another cup of coffee and stepped out on the porch to take his favorite spot and watch the activity on the St. Johns River.

Mary C. was taking a shower and checking her body for ticks. She had found one on her arm when she was out on her land and wanted to be sure there were no more of the nasty insects on her body or in her hair. She touched herself with a soapy hand when the warm water ran down her body. She was hoping the water would be hot enough to create the smoky steam that once brought Hawk to her in the same shower. She knew it was probably her hopeful imagination but strange things had happened in that house when it came to the dead. Mary C. thought Hawk's appearance may have something to do with Mr. King's house and the magic carousel. When Hawk did not appear she pleasured herself with her fingers and the palm of her hand. She actually moaned with delight as her body fluids joined the warm water. It helped clear her mind.

Mr. King was still sitting on the porch when Mary C. walked to the front of the house and looked out of the screen. "John, you might want to take a shower to be sure no ticks came home with ya."

He turned to see Mary C. in her white robe, with her wet hair, her bare feet and muscular legs. It was a great sight for any man. "I think I'll do that. Good idea."

Mary C. went to her bedroom to dry her hair and get dressed. She had plans to go visit Miss Carolyn later in the evening. She heard the shower down the hall as she took off the white robe and tossed it on the bed. Mary C. had no body length oval mirrors to look at herself. There was a small mirror above the dresser. She could only see herself from the waist up. Mary C. loved a big mirror but she would have to make do with what she had for now. She turned to her side and impressed herself with the way her breasts still stood firm and at attention. She went up on her toes to get a better look at her flat stomach. Her calf muscles bulged when she went up on her toes. She could not see her buttocks, but a good slap and squeeze told her all was tight and firm down south.

Mary C. pushed her breasts together forming a deep cleavage and then pinched both her nipples with her thumb and index finger. Mary C. laid back on the bed with her feet flat on the bed and knees bent. She opened her legs as wide as she could and let her fingers and palm of her hand go to work again. Mary C.'s sexual juices were boiling. She was wet before her fingers were inside her body.

It only took thirty seconds for her muscles to tighten and release her fluids again. Her mind was more than clear. She decided to get dressed, go see Miss Carolyn and go into Jacksonville Beach for an evening on the town. When she sat up on the edge of the bed she saw the Croom twins looking into the bedroom window. They had climbed up the outside back stairs and were watching her from the top balcony. She covered herself with a pillow and moved toward the window. She watched them run down the back steps. Mary C. would not tell Mr. King.

Miss Margaret turned to the front door of the store when the bell rang. Her sad eyes fell upon Robert Fussell's bloody face and neck. "Oh, Robert, what happened?"

Robert took a deep breath. "I had a little problem out on the rocks and I need some help to get this hook out of my lip." He poked his lip out so she could see the hook.

"Oh dear, I've seen this before. We have to clip off the end and pull it out so the barb does not tear the lip."

Mr. Fussell knew she was right. "Yes ma'am. I have wire cutters here in my pocket. I tried to do it in the truck mirror, but my hand was shakin' too much. I need some help."

Miss Margaret stepped closer. "I can't promise my hands will be too steady, but I can try. You have to get that thing out of your lip."

Mr. King found no ticks on his body during his shower. As she walked down the hall from the bathroom to his bedroom Mary C. yelled from downstairs. "I'm goin' out to see Miss Carolyn, and then over to the Beach. I'll see ya later."

Mr. King knew she was gone for the night. "Be careful. See ya when ya get here."

He stepped to his bedroom window and watched Mary C. leave the porch and climb into her trusty Ford Falcon. Mr. King was puzzled when Mary C. drove away in the direction toward the ferry slip. He thought she was going to Miss Margaret's store at first. He watched the Falcon drive past the store and turn right in the direction of the oak tree and the sand hill. The thought crossed his mind that perhaps she was returning to the scene of her most recent crime. Mr. King dried his hair and got dressed.

Mary C. did slow the car down as she drove past the sand hill and the grape arbor. She did not think about visiting the crime scene. Mary C. stopped the car and looked under the grape arbor. She was looking for Chuck and Buck. They were not there.

The bell on the door rang again. Miss Margaret and Mr. Fussell turned to see who was entering the store. It was Mr. King. He saw the blood on Mr. Fussell.

"Robert, what have you done?" He then saw the hook. "Oh Lord, that really looks painful."

Mr. Fussell grinned the best he could. "What give you that idea, John?"

"Just a hunch, I guess."

"Actually, it's rather numb at this point. Miss Margaret was just getting ready to help me get it out." He held up the wire cutter pliers.

Mr. King took the cutters from Mr. Fussell's hand. "In your present condition you won't believe this but it's your lucky day. I am an expert at hook removal. I've pulled them out of many a catfish in my time. Just about the same spot, too."

Mr. Fussell knew a good hook pulling joke when he heard one, but it hurt too bad to smile and laughing was out of the question.

It was easy to see the relief on Miss Margaret's face when she realized she would not have to do the operation on Mr. Fussell's face. She was more than happy to turn the responsibility over to the expert, Mr. John King. She wasn't sure about the catfish comment.

"Are you sure it's the same when taking a hook out of a human?"

Mr. King tried to keep a straight face. "I don't see why it would be any different." He demonstrated in the air with the pliers. "You just take hold and twist it out like this."

Even Mr. Fussell had to close his eyes at Mr. King's rendition of a proper hook removal. Miss Margaret put her hand over her mouth as if she might scream. Mr. King stepped to Mr. Fussell.

"I need to clip off the one end and slide it out away from the barb."

Mr. Robert Fussell grimaced in pain as Mr. King pressed the wire cutters together and took hold of the end of the fish hook. The pressure caused pain but Mr. Fussell knew it was necessary as part of the removal process. He felt the most pain when the end of the hook was clipped off and Mr. King pulled the hook out, making sure the barb did not touch the skin. Miss Margaret did not watch the procedure. Mr. King handed the hook to his patient.

"You want to keep this? Make a necklace?"

As Mr. Fussell took the hook from Mr. King, Miss Margaret poured the peroxide on a white cloth and wiped Mr. Fussell's mouth and neck, cleaning off the blood. She was gentle when she moved the cloth over his lip. The hole from the hook bubbled with foam from the cleaning process of the peroxide. That was always a good thing when it came to cuts and scratches.

Mr. King was too curious to keep his thought to himself. "I know you probably don't feel like talkin' right now, but what the hell happened?"

Miss Margaret stopped her nurse work and moved away from Mr. Fussell anticipating his answer. Mr. Fussell knew what to say first. He was a true gentleman. "Thank you, Miss Margaret. Thank you, John."

Miss Margaret smiled. "You're most welcome, Robert. I hope you're going to be okay. That's a nasty hole in your lip."

Mr. King was still curious. "You're welcome. I'm glad I was here to help. Now, how in the world did this happen?"

"John, I hate to think this, but it was done on purpose by one of those twins." Mr. King's face turned red as Mr. Fussell continued with his thoughts about the evil ones. "One of 'em hit me in the face with his line earlier in the day. He almost caught me in the eye that time but I was lucky. I yelled for them to be careful. The boy seemed sorry and I left it at that. One time could be an honest accident, but not a second time. When the hook caught my lip I knew it was intentional."

Mr. King's blood was boiling as he listened to Mr. Fussell and knew that he was correct about the boy hurting him intentionally. Mr. Fussell went on as Miss Margaret and Mr. King listened. "The boy even tried to pull the pole so he could rip the hook out once he realized it did stick in me. I had to hold on to the line so he couldn't pull on it."

Miss Margaret made a face and had to speak up. "That's awful, Robert. Do you really think they wanted to hurt you?" Mr. King did not give Mr. Fussell time to answer. "Ya damn right, they wanted to hurt him. They spend their days hurtin' as many people and animals as they can. Those two are a plague on Mayport. Somebody else is gonna get hurt bad with those two runnin' crazy around here."

Miss Margaret did not know how to respond to Mr. King's harsh comments about the Croom twins. Mr. Fussell had more to say. "When I got to my truck they had flattened all four tires and broke both the tail lights. I have to go deal with that, now. This was not one of my better days in Mayport."

Mr. King was mad. "We need to go see their daddy and then I'll help you get your truck goin' or at least get you back home."

The threesome turned to the front door when the bell rang once again. Miss Margaret smiled when she saw her youngest daughter, Sofia, walk into the store. Miss Margaret was surprised but happy to see her.

"Sofia, how nice of you to come over. Are you all right?"

Sofia's voice was low and soft. "Yes, ma'am. I'm fine. I thought you might need some help or would want to take a break."

Miss Margaret loved Sofia. Mr. King greeted the young beauty.

"Hello, Sofia."

"Hello, Mr. King."

Mr. Robert Fussell was captivated by Sofia's natural beauty. For some reason he had never seen or met Sofia on his trips to Mayport. He nodded but had no words. Miss Margaret made the introduction.

"Robert, this is my youngest, Sofia. Sofia, this is Mr. Fussell. He's a fireman in Jacksonville."

Sofia reached out to shake Mr. Fussell's hand. "Nice to meet you, sir." Sofia looked directly at his swollen and cut lip. "Oh, my, you've hurt yourself."

Sofia's long blonde hair, long legs, ice-blue eyes, straight white teeth, flawless skin and firm perfect body would render any man speechless when they first met her. Robert Fussell was no different. He just smiled. Miss Margaret had seen his symptoms many times when she introduced her beautiful daughter to men of all ages. She saved Mr. Fussell from fumbling his words.

"Robert got a fish hook stuck in his lip and Mr. King just got it out."

Sofia stepped closer to Mr. Fussell. Things like that did not bother her anymore. She had seen enough painful things and had a new attitude about it.

"Oh my, that does look like it hurts."

To add to her aura, Sofia smelled great, too. Mr. Fussell's nose and senses were filled with the young woman. "It's pretty numb, now. I'm sure I'll feel it more, later tonight."

Miss Margaret smiled and addressed her daughter. "There's some stock in the back I was trying to get out on the shelves if you want to help. Things okay at the house?"

"Yes, ma'am. I'll get the stock out." Sofia turned to Mr. Fussell. "Nice meeting you, sir. I'm sorry you got hurt."

Mr. Fussell smiled a swollen lip crooked smile. "Nice to meet you, too."

Sofia turned to Mr. King. "Always nice to see you, Mr. King. Any new ghosts, lately?"

"Nice to see you, too. And there's always new noises in my halls."

Sofia smiled once more and went to the back stockroom. Mr. Fussell turned to Miss Margaret. "Thank you so much for your help and kindness."

Miss Margaret stepped to Mr. Fussell and hugged him gently. "You drive careful, now and get some rest when you get home."

"I'm off work the next few days. I think I'll stay away from the jetties for now."

Mr. King still wanted to go to the Croom house. He

looked at Mr. Fussell. "Let's make that visit we discussed and then I'll help you with your car." He turned to Miss Margaret. "Will you call Chip Parman out at Big Chief and ask him to send a tow truck out to the Little Jetties in about thirty minutes? We'll meet em' out there."

"Of course."You two be careful with those two boys."

Chuck and Buck stopped walking when they saw the Ford Falcon rolling toward them. They had sat in the Falcon that awful day and watched their older brother Joe being killed by the devil dog. The memory flashed pounding their brains made both boys sick to their stomachs. They were mesmerized when they saw the car. Neither one noticed Mary C. at the wheel. They both just stood there like they were in a trance as the car rolled up next to them. Mary C. was surprised they did not run when she stopped the car only a few feet away. She rolled down the window, but did not get out of the car and kept the engine running. The twins still stared at the car. Mary C. brought them back to the reality of the moment.

"That was a bad day, wasn't it boys?"

Chuck and Buck came back mentally at the same time. They were identical twins and they were not afraid. They looked at each other and then at Mary C. Chuck broke the silence.

"We hate that car. How can you ride in that car?"

"It's my car. Joe liked this car. The dog killed Joe not the car."

"We know that was your dog."

Mary C. nodded her head. "I killed it."

Buck shook his head. "Too late."

Chuck walked to the opened window of the car. Mary C. was glad she stayed in the Falcon. He was not afraid at all. Mary C. did not like the feeling running through her blood.

"You boys know you could get killed for sneakin' around and peeping into people's bedroom windows. Folks can shoot a peeping tom and won't get in trouble at all. I'm gonna shoot both y'all if you come near my room again. I just wanted to come find y'all and give ya that warnin' so when I splatter ya brains all over the place, it won't be a surprise to ya. You two need to get on home before I do it right now." Mary C. held up her favorite weapon of choice so the boys could see she had her pump action shotgun with her.

Chuck stepped back away from the window. Buck's eyes widened when he saw the shotgun. They did not respond and were afraid of Mary C.'s threat and demonstration of fire power.

Mary C. put the car in gear and pushed down the gas pedal. The Falcon moved slowly away from the twins. She looked into her rearview mirror and saw them both making nasty hand gestures in her direction. Mary C. thought that if they waited for her to leave to be disrespectful, then she must have put the scare in them that she wanted. Mr. King saw the Falcon as it turned onto the main road leading out of Mayport. He and Mr. Fussell were on their way to visit the Croom house.

Big Joe Croom was working on one of his gill nets when Mr. King's Chevy rolled into his front yard. The twins were playing on a tire swing that was hanging from a limb of an oak tree to the left of the house. They were recovering from their encounter with Mary C. and her shotgun. As usual, Pee Wee was helping his father mend the net.

Big Joe Croom had lost his wife, his oldest son, and drank far too much heavy liquor. He had to take care of Pee Wee and the twins. Pee Wee was a pleasure. Chuck and Buck added to his consumption of alcohol. The car stopped and the twin's eyes widened when Mr. King and their latest victim, Mr. Fussell, stepped out of the Chevy. They remained standing at the swing but they watched the two visitors.

Big Joe and Pee Wee stopped working on the net. Big Joe knew something was wrong. He looked at the twins and they both ran into the woods next to the house. Big Joe couldn't recall the last time Mr. King had been in his front yard and he did not know the man with him. As the two men approached he was compelled to speak up.

"What's wrong, John? Why are my boys runnin' away and hidin' in the woods?"

Sofia walked out of the stockroom carrying a box full of merchandise to place on the store shelves. Miss Margaret wanted to talk to her.

"What about your sisters, how are things at the house?"

Sofia was different. She would pull no punches. "The house is empty, mother. They're all gone. I'm sure you knew they would leave. There's no one there."

Miss Margaret took a deep breath as if she did not believe her youngest. She stared at her daughter. Sofia would not allow her mother to act like everything was fine.

"They're gone."

Miss Margaret lowered her head and broke the stare. "And you? Why are you still here?"

Sofia took her own deep breath. "I'm still too scared to go. But, I'm getting stronger every time we go through something awful. I'm sure I'll be gone one day, too. I'm also here because I love you." She turned and began stocking the shelves.

Mr. Fussell had told his story and showed his damaged lip to Big Joe Croom. Mr. King added his story about his disrespectful encounters with the two boys. Big Joe reeked of hard liquor as he listened to his two visitors. He did not comment while both men talked. When they finished, his response had no substance.

"I'm sorry about your lip, mister. But it's hard to believe one of the boys could hook you on purpose. It would probably take a hundred tries to actually hook someone if you were trying to do it. And you really can't say you saw them do that stuff to your car, now can ya?" He turned to Mr. King. "I'm sorry they were disrespectful, John. They've been like that since we lost their mama and Joe. I'll see they're punished."

Mr. King and Mr. Fussell knew his words were empty. They had no reason to remain there. They both turned to

walk back to the car without saying a word. Big Joe watched
them walk away. When Mr. King opened the car door he
could not leave without expressing his thoughts.

"Joe, we're all sad about your losses this past year, no
one but you knows what you've been goin' through, but
those two boys are gonna hurt somebody really bad and folks
are gonna blame you for not makin' 'em behave. The man's
got a hole in his lip, four flat tires and two broken tail lights
and you want proof your boys did it. The real sad thing is
you know they did it. You keep makin' excuses for 'em and
somethin' bad is in the future for you and those two."

Big Joe didn't like Mr. King's tone. "That sounds like a
threat, John."

"Take it anyway you want, Joe. It's just a fact."

As they left the Croom's front yard, they passed a
wooded section of the dirt road leading away from the house.
Mr. King saw a figure to the left on the road on his side. He
knew it was one of the Croom twins even though the boy
wore a ski-mask over his head. Mr. Fussell had a masked
man on his side of the road as well. The boys were running
in the woods like wild Indians getting ready to attack the
stage coach. It was unnerving at first but as fast as they
appeared they were gone. Mr. King looked at Mr. Fussell as
he stopped the car and prepared to pull out onto the main
road back to Mayport. Mr. Fussell looked out the car
window. "Those are some strange young boys there."

Mr. King did not have time to respond. The voice of one
of the twins filled the air around them. It was as if the boy
was sitting in the truck with them. It was an unnatural voice.

"Come she come."

"What letter she come bye?"

"PC." There was an eerie silence. And then both boys
yelled "Pine cones."

At that moment Mr. King's mint condition 1955 Ford
was the target of what seemed to be hundreds of pine cones.
Not the fully opened, light weight version, but the rock hard,

yet to open, still green version. They were bouncing off of the hood and top of the truck five to ten at a time. Each cone that connected formed a dent or scratch mark on the body of the car. The barrage was over in about thirty seconds. The boys were gone. The damage was done.

Mr. King pushed down on the gas pedal and pulled the car into the open road. Mr. Fussell's body was slammed against the passenger door as Mr. King turned the car around and headed back toward the Croom house. He left a cloud of dust on the road with another cloud following him back down the dirt road. What a day Mr. Fussell had already been through and now he was smack dab in the middle of a family feud. All he wanted to do was get a tow truck out at the Little Jetties and get his truck and throbbing lip home. The car came to a sliding halt in Joe Croom's front yard.

Joe Croom stepped off of his front porch when Mr. King jumped out of the car and came storming toward him. Joe Croom was a big man, but more of a coward than he wanted to be. He had fear in his eyes as Mr. King approached him.

"What is it, John? What's wrong?"

Mr. King was wild eyed with his head on a swivel as he looked for the twins. "Where are they, Joe? Get 'em out here, right now."

Mr. Croom looked from side to side. "I ain't seen 'em, John, I swear. They ain't come back."

Mr. King turned to his damaged car. "Look what they did to my car. They waited for us at the end of the road. They ambushed us like wild crazy Indians, Joe. They had ski masks over their heads. What's wrong with those boys, Joe? Somethin' bad, I think."

Mr. King did not wait for Mr. Croom to respond. "And please don't say, 'how do we know it was them?' I don't think I could take a question like that from you. It was them and you better find the money to fix my car. I'll let you know how much that will be in a day or so." Mr. King turned away and walked back to the car. Joe Croom had no words.

CHAPTER THREE

Jason, Billy and Rebecca had been at the Giant's Motel for a few days. It was different there. Everything does change, like it or not. Big Bob, Beulla, Helga and Ana Kara were the only ones left from the original circus group. With the magic and hypnotic voices of Ming and Ling no longer captivating the local audiences, the lounge was near empty each night. Beulla did play her rock-n-roll songs on her piano Friday and Saturday nights, but to very few customers. Ana Kara danced for a group of local bikers when they came around, but not on a regular basis. Ana knew she should probably leave and use her talents elsewhere, but she wasn't young anymore and was afraid of failure or ridicule.

Ming and Ling had both fallen in love with the same man and decided to make Mr. Lucky Lane a happy man. He was a local tomato farmer and no doubt the happiest man in Ruskin, Florida. Helga had commented that she would really like to see those twins go to work on one man. It would be well worth the ticket price.

The area Southern Baptist congregation frowned on one man having two women in his bed. The non-church goers said that Lucky was finally living up to his name. Helga had called on the threesome a number of times hoping to catch them during sexual activity. She did love to watch but Helga was a much better participant than she was a spectator. She had even invited the twins and their man to spend a night in the carousel room, hoping she could find a way to watch them or join in. Helga desperately missed the excitement and sexual activity of her true love, the midget, Tom Thumb. She liked Jason and knew he was open to her sexual prowess. Each woman he was involved with had a different type of beauty. She thought Rebecca Coolie was a rare find and was attracted to the young woman in the worst way. She fantasized a sexual threesome with Jason and Rebecca.

Another reason the crowd had gone from the motel lounge was because of the violent death of Grady the Lobster Boy. He was one of the few original circus people who did not stay at the Giant's Motel with the others. The stories of his abuse of his family and his brutal death at the hands of teenagers, brought a spotlight on the circus people as more than odd, evil, and deranged. The thought was that you never knew when such people would explode on normal folks. They became freaks and outcasts once again. With fewer workers and less money coming in for upkeep, the motel was deteriorating around them. Jason was concerned when Big Bob told him how he recognized two men who came by asking questions about Tom Green. Jason knew his thought should be on his son, Billy, but he did not want Tom Green to be hurt or captured.

Jason and Rebecca had a room together. Beulla, she pronounced it Bee-ulla, had taken on the motherly role of caring for Billy. She loved her role as the caretaker of the child. Jason loved the fact he had Rebecca "Milkduds" Coolie and all her sexual talents and attributes to himself. It was a special treat he did not expect. Rebecca was like the other women in Jason's life. They loved him and would always remember the special times they shared with him. Jason was captivated with Rebecca because she would do anything to please him sexually. He was enjoying his time with Rebecca.

Mr. King stood outside his car at the Little Jetties while

Robert Fussell talked to Chip Parman from the Big Chief Tire Company. Mr. Parman brought all the equipment they would need to repair the four flat tires on the spot. Mr. Parman always seemed to go out of his way to help the locals. Mr. King would not leave Mr. Fussell until he was on his way home.

Margie spent the day in her room thinking of what she would do next. Going home at the moment was out of the question. She lay on the bed thinking about too many things. She tried to wipe Jason out of her head but he always seemed to work his way into her thoughts. She wished she had the carousel with her and could dream the time away. Margie was addicted to Jason, the carousel, the oak tree and sex.

Rebecca "Milkduds" Coolie stepped out of the shower in the room at the Giant's Motel and wrapped a towel around her wet and unbelievable body. Jason was sitting on the edge of the bed waiting for her to join him. Rebecca had no inhibitions, what so ever, when it came to being naked and having sexual relations. Her sexual drive and knowledge was most unnatural for a woman so young. Jason had been with many women but he knew Rebecca was far sexually superior to all of them. He also knew she would please anyone who would take care of her. Rebecca knew how to use her body and talents.

Jason was wearing only his skivvies. She dropped the towel to the floor, exposing her huge firm breasts and her hard thick body to match. Rebecca knelt down in front of Jason, pulling his skivvies down and taking them off of his ankles. Rebecca held Jason's excitement in her hand. She loved the way he reacted to her. She then used her lips for his first of many pleasures to come. It was impossible to tire of Rebecca and what she brought to bed.

The noises around Margie's room at the Sand Pipe Hotel had stopped. She cracked open the door and decided she would change her clothes and see what was happening in the area of Jacksonville Beach called the Board Walk. She had heard there would be music and dancing at the Band Shell.

Margie was a woman on her own with a great deal to offer the man or men who were fortunate enough to catch her fancy. Margie looked into the full-length mirror on the bathroom door. She wore tight black pedal-pushers showing her calf muscles. Her wide collar white calypso shirt was tied at the waist exposing her flat stomach and navel. She pulled the shirt open so three inches of breast cleavage would be visible for anyone interested in taking a closer look. When Margie stepped out into that hotel hallway she was a female force to be reckoned with. She was still afraid but she wanted to be on her own. The evening hours were approaching and the lights of the Board Walk would be illuminating the sky.

Margie's evening stroll down the Jacksonville Beach Board Walk was more than a beautiful woman taking a walk near the ocean. It was a coming out moment for a newly independent woman with a fire in her belly and excitement in her immediate future. She knew men and women were both watching her as she made her way down the wooden slats of the old section of the Board Walk. Margie did not realize it, but she began to carry herself in the same fashion as Mary C. did when she was out to entice.

Jason lifted Rebecca's head and ended her oral assault. He wanted her to sit across him with his feet on the floor and her legs around him. Rebecca read his action like a book and moved over him, placing his manhood inside her. As Jason sunk deep into her, there was a knock at the door. Both their heads turned toward the door. They were silent for a few seconds and then there was a second knock. The voice they heard surprised Rebecca but not Jason. It was Helga. She was like a bloodhound when it came to sexual relations in the vicinity.

"I'm sorry to bother you two, but I was hopin' I could watch."

Rebecca's beautiful eyes opened wide. "What did she say?"

Jason did not answer her question as he moved Rebecca from her sitting position across him. He put his skivvies back on, left Rebecca in the bed and walked toward the door. Rebecca was not sure she wanted Jason to open the door and allow the strange and tall circus woman to join them in the room. However, she did realize she had no say in allowing Helga into the room. Even thought they had all been kind to her she still felt strange being surrounded by the former Big Top oddities. Rebecca did feel safe as long as Jason was with her. Jason knew Helga wanted to watch him and Milkduds during their sexual activity. He really didn't mind and he knew Rebecca would do whatever he wanted. Jason was actually intrigued and interested in what Helga might bring to the experience. He opened the door.

Helga looked into the room and could see Rebecca sitting on the bed holding a pillow up to hide her naked frontal exposure. Her football sized breasts were bulging up as she pressed the pillow to her body. Helga could not contain herself.

"Oh Jason! She is a true beauty. This one may very well be the answer to all our prayers."

Jason had no idea what Helga meant but he smiled and allowed her to walk past him. Helga walked directly to the foot of the bed. Rebecca continued to hide her body.

Jason knew what Helga wanted so he motioned for Rebecca to take the pillow away. Without hesitation Rebecca tossed the pillow back onto the bed. She stood there completely naked. The sight of Rebecca's incredible body took Helga's breath away. She talked while her eyes scanned Rebecca from head to toe.

"I have seen the most beautiful bodies from all over the world. I was once one of the most sought after. None that I have seen come close to you, my dear. You are a physical treasure. You would have walked with the gods on Olympus. They would have burned Troy for you as well. If Helga had what you have she would be the richest woman on the Earth."

Rebecca was not sure she understood all of it but she liked what the tall Amazon Woman had to say. She remained naked, sat down on the edge of the bed and wanted to hear more. Jason sat down in a chair to watch the two women's relationship progress. Helga continued.

"I don't mean to scare you and I'm not as strange as you may think. I was awkward and too tall when I was young. A true freak, if you will. I was ugly and did not develop this body until I was in my early twenties. By that time I had been a side show in the circus for five years. I was the tallest woman, but not the Amazon Woman."

Rebecca sat on the bed and did not cover herself as Helga went on. "Then it seemed right out of nowhere, my body changed almost overnight. All of my womanly attributes developed to match my height. I was no longer the skinny, ugly girl. I was the Amazon Woman. Men desired me and would give me things to allow them to touch me. They paid me to be with them. They wanted me, but did not want to stay with me. It was my circus background and my past as a circus sideshow attraction. They were willing to bed me and pay me, but they did not want to take a circus freak home to their mothers. I was not smart. Why did it matter so much if they left me? They were using me but I wanted love. I didn't realize that if I used them too, I could have anything I wanted. I was a stupid young woman." Helga looked at Jason. "Helga talks too much, don't you think?"

Jason smiled. "You always have interesting things to say." He looked at Rebecca. "We have all had interesting lives. We're all oddballs."

Helga smiled at Jason's philosophical moment. "Yes, we are all oddballs." She looked at Rebecca. Helga loved Jason but her mind had been working overtime from the moment she saw Jason's new lady friend.

"I became sad and discouraged that these men would lay with me for hours, even days but they would leave me when they had enough." She looked at Jason. "Tom was always there for me. He was proud to be seen with me and to walk beside me. We went places and had great times. Sure people stared but that was nothing new for us. We had been on display all our lives." She smiled. "Now, I know he was a nasty little devil but he could sure satisfy a woman. He used his talents on me because no other woman would have him. That was their loss. We satisfied each other everyday and most of the time more than once. I miss my little man with his tiny hands and big sword. We were both true warriors." Helga sat down next to the still naked Rebecca. "Helga wants to leave this place and find the good life again. We could both be rich women if you let me teach you what I know." Helga looked at Jason. "He loves you in his own way, but he cannot stay with you. There have been many before you and there will be many after you. Only one will have him in the end."

Jason loved the way the circus people talked. He had since he arrived at the Giant's Motel the first time. Rebecca looked at Jason and then back at Helga.

"I have always understood about Jason and other women. I know it is a day-to-day relationship. I will always be his if he wants me."

Helga nodded her head and looked at Jason. "But isn't he exciting on that daily basis?" Rebecca smiled and looked at Jason. Helga had more. "I am an intruder, hoping to watch you two together. I'm aware that such a desire adds to my freak status. I am hoping that eventually you will allow me to join you and teach you what Helga has learned about the human body and pleasure." Helga reached out and touched Rebecca's hand. "You have the attitude I should have had years ago. I could have been the richest woman in the world. With what you have and what I know, we can both be the richest women in the world."

Jason did not care about who became rich or not. He was excited. He stood up, pulled off his white skivvies and walked to the bed with his manhood standing at attention. Helga's eyes widened as he moved past her. After Tom Thumb's death she had only pleasured herself and was craving to be with a partner or partners. She was over-whelmed.

"Helga can join you?"

Jason smiled at the wide eyed Rebecca. "Of course."

Helga took off her blouse and laid it on the chair. Her body was still rock hard and her black skin was tight and smooth. Her breasts were big and round with black nipples. When she dropped her pants, she exposed her clean shaved private area. Rebecca had never seen such a sight. Jason was prepared. He had seen Helga's smooth area once before. Helga walked to the bathroom.

"Please begin. I have to take a shower and be clean for you both."

Margie looked out into the darkness over the Atlantic Ocean as a salt scented breeze touched her face and moved her hair. She could see the white foam of the waves touch the shore in the darkness. The fun sounds of the Penny Arcade and the young girls screaming on the Board Walk amusement rides made her smile as she turned to begin her evening.

With Helga in the shower, Rebecca resumed her oral pleasuring for Jason. It was as if they were both waiting for Helga to bring her magic to the bed.

Robert Fussell was glad he was driving away from Mayport. It would be a day he would not forget. Mr. King was back home and drinking another cup of coffee. He was alone and trying to calm the anger inside him ignited by the evil deeds of the twins. He stepped out onto his front porch ready to relax as best he could, but the sight of this damaged car added to his discomfort.

Helga's black skin glistened as she walked out of the bathroom patting her body dry with a towel. She dropped the towel and stood there so her two new students could see what she had to offer them. She was a big woman. Her words were music to Jason's ears.

"Helga is here to please you both today. There will be other days for pleasing Helga."

Officers David Boos and Paul Short sat at a table in the

Coffee Cup Restaurant in Ruskin, Florida. They were having an early dinner and looking for information to the whereabouts of the fugitive, Tom Green. The waitress was an older woman like most of the women working at the popular restaurant and pie house. It was obvious the workers had been part of the scenery there for some time. It was one of those places where once you got a job there, you stayed. Good working conditions, good tips and plenty of customers usually contributes to the existence of loyal employees. The waitress brought the menu's pot roast special to the lawmen.

"Here ya go fellas. Pipin' hot."

David Boos looked at her name tag. "Thanks Buck. It sure smells good."

Buck smiled her, "Don't forget my tip" smile. "You gentlemen enjoy your meal, but be sure to leave some room for a slice of pie. You can't eat at the Coffee Cup without havin' a big piece of pie. Any selection you make will be a great culinary experience for ya."

Both men had to smile at Buck's deep southern drawl, choice of words and beehive hairdo. They had experienced a slice of pie there before so they knew she was telling the truth. They liked talking to Buck but they both had other things on their minds. Buck was pouring Paul Short some more sweet tea.

"Buck, we're police officers. We're looking for a black man named Tom Green. We know he lives in the area. He's a fugitive and has been on the run for many years. Do you know that name?"

They had no idea Buck had met another lawman a year ago who was looking for Tom Green. Jake Shackleford had spent a night in her trailer just before he died. She put the pitcher of sweet tea on the table. Her answer surprised both men.

"Of course I know that name. I'll bet all the people in this room know that name. Everyone knows about y'all, too and why you're here. We actually drew straws in the back to see who had to wait on y'all. I lost. We don't want y'all here, but since ya are, ya might as well have a good meal and a big piece of pie. Folks don't fare too well when they come lookin' for Tom Green. Last time a lawman asked me about Tom Green, he got killed that very day."

David Boos stopped eating his pot roast. He considered her last statement as a subtle threat. Buck got tickled and laughed out loud. "Oh no, mister, we ain't gonna poison y'all or nothin'. Our cook wouldn't ruin a good pot roast just to kill somebody. That was not a threat at all just a fact."

David Boos smiled a nervous grin. He wasn't so sure about the pot roast. Buck had the smile of an angel but it was obvious she had a touch of the devil in her as well. He put his fork down.

"Do you know where he is?"

"No sir, I don't. And you do understand that if I did, I wouldn't tell y'all anyway?"

"No, I don't think I do understand. Why is that?"

"Now, you two don't get me wrong. I ain't got a lot of black friends. Don't want none. We got a black cook here in the kitchen. She's been here twenty-five years. I like her but she ain't never been to my house. Tom Green ain't never been to my house before either, but ain't me or nobody around here gonna tell you two bounty hunters where he is even if they do know. Besides, he ain't been around her in a year or so, maybe longer."

Buck walked away from the table. The two bounty hunters looked at each other. David Boos shook his head.

"What's the real story with these people? This place is crawlin' with Confederate Flag wavin', clan supportin', back woods red-necks but none of 'em will give up one old black man. What's goin' on around here?"

Paul Short nodded. "Well, ya know that boy Jason treats him like he's family. He's probably a good man and found himself in the wrong place at the wrong time. We've both seen that happen before."

David Boos knew the crime. "He killed the damn sheriff

in East Mayport about twenty years ago. After runnin' and hidin' out for twenty years he shows up in Mayport to pay his respects and attend an old friend's funeral. As he's leavin' town, he just happens to kill another lawman and he runs again. We should have taken him back when we were here last time."

Paul Short had to remind his partner of that past situation. "We would both be dead if we had tried to take him back last time. Maybe he don't deserve to be punished. Maybe he had to kill those people, Mr. Butler, too."

David Boos nodded. "I know we've both always felt that. We've talked about it before. But now we've got a bunch of money and even more if we take him back. And if he's been wrongly accused or not, he is a fugitive with an open warrant out for his capture and arrest."

The meal was over. They did not order a slice of pie. Buck returned to the table. They both stood up. "You gents sure you don't want a slice of that banana cream pie? It's a slice of heaven. I'll fix it myself if you're afraid somebody else might spit in it."

They both shook their heads at the thought, vision and possibility the colorful Buck had created for them. David Boos paid the bill and Paul Short left her a generous tip. As they approached the door Buck saw the tip on the table. She picked it up and walked out into the parking lot where they were approaching the car.

"Thank you very much, gentlemen. You didn't have to be so kind. I'm sorry I wasn't very helpful to your cause. I am glad I picked the shortest straw."

Paul Short had to ask her. "Can you at least tell us why he's so protected? This ain't no Yankee town we're in, now is it?"

Buck smiled and understood what he was saying. She took a deep breath and considered the tip they had left her.

"He gives all he has and takes or wants nothin' in return. He gives and expects no payback. I'm sure you two don't know about him running into that house and rescuing Mrs.

Marshall while it was burnin' down around her. She was bedridden at the time and 'ol Tom carried her big butt out into the front yard. Tom burned his leg real bad, but Mrs. Marshall didn't have a scratch on her. She did get a little bruised up when the fireman dropped the stretcher they were carrying her on. She's still alive today. I'm sure she ain't gonna help y'all find him." Buck hesitated for just a second or so but had more to offer the two lawmen.

"Then there was that time when Mr. Long's pitbull went after little Cindy Hoffman. She wasn't but about four years old. We all hated that dog. It was just a matter of time before he went crazy. They always do. He would have killed her if Tom wasn't there to save her. They both got bit. Tom's was the worst. They did have to fix little Cindy's ear. It does look a little different than the other ear. Cindy's bite marks healed up real good as she got older. Hell, twelve years later she was picked as the Homecoming Queen at the high school. I'll bet that would have never happened if Tom hadn't got that dog off of her. I'll also bet the Hoffman family won't be helpin' y'all find ol' tom."

Buck stopped again and stared at the two officers for a few seconds. She thought they might have something to say.

"Would you gentlemen like to hear more?"

They were both intrigued. David Boos nodded for them both. "Please continue if there's more to tell."

Buck smiled. She was on a roll. "When Sam Conner's house was the only one leveled by the one and only tornado that ever touched down in Ruskin, Tom was the first man to go and help Sam clean up the mess. He brought all his field hands and they worked until the job was done. Then they helped Sam rebuild the house when they was needed." Buck knew she had the lawmen's attention.

"I think I'll leave you two with one last bit of information. When those two drifters robbed and beat old man Haley and left him for dead at the store, Tom and his field hands tracked 'em down and found 'em on the beach over on Anna Maria Island. It only took two days for Tom to find 'em. He brought back Mr. Haley's money. Nobody asked what happened to the two drifters. Nobody cared. He might be black but he's an angel. Tom Green is a black angel." Buck was finished. "You gentlemen have a nice stay here in our little town. And do come back to the Coffee Cup if you're ever back this way again." It was interesting how Buck was sure they were leaving the area as if she knew something they did not.

Jason was sitting in the chair watching the Amazon Woman work her sexual magic on Rebecca "Milkduds" Coolie. Helga had drained him of all his juices and he was more than happy to be a spectator. He could see that Rebecca was not interested in him at all. She had the same look about her when they were with Nadine Porter at the Night Moves honky tonk. It was becoming obvious that Rebecca liked being sexual with men and women, but if she had to make a choice between the two a man would be her second selection. He smiled and continued his observation.

Helga played Rebecca's incredible body like it was keys on a piano and Helga was a concert pianist. Jason only allowed Helga to handle Rebecca for about twenty minutes before he was compelled to join them again. He could just take so much visual pleasure and stimulation. It wasn't like him but he felt a little twinge of jealousy. Rebecca affected him differently than the others. He knew Helga's prediction was correct and he would not be with Rebecca very long. He also knew she would be with him whenever the opportunity presented itself. He joined the two newly acquainted sexual goddesses. His cup runneth over. It always did.

Officers David Boos and Paul Short were standing in front of their room at the Apollo Beach Motel. A man approached them from a poorly lighted area between two buildings. Paul Short put his hand on the handle of his concealed pistol. He knew when it was time to be alert and on guard. Buck's, "I won't let 'em spit in the pie", attitude added to the "be on the alert" status. Paul Short stepped away from his partner as the man came closer. When he walked into the light he was an exceptionally shinny man, with tanned skin, dirty clothes, few teeth and serious tobacco stains on the teeth he had left. He wore no shoes and his feet were black from the dirt or any other thing he stepped into. Paul Short decided the man was close enough.

"Hold it right there, mister. You don't need to keep comin' at us like you are. It makes me nervous."

The dirty man stopped. "Oh, sorry sir. I don't mean no harm. I thought maybe I could help you fellas. I heard y'all was lookin' for somebody."

David Boos did not like the nasty man. "If you know we're looking for somebody, you must know who it is."

The man smiled an awful nasty grin. "Everybody knows who you're lookin' for. I was here when you looked for him the last time. Why you come back here?"

Paul Short had heard enough. He grabbed the man and pushed him against the wall of the building. "I'm tired of these games. I ask the questions you sack of shit. If you don't have the answers get the hell away from us. Quit wasting our time." He released the man and stepped back to the car.

The dirty man smiled again. "Y'all pretty frustrated, ain't ya boys?"

That was it for Paul Short. He ran and slammed the man to the ground placing his pistol to his head. Through angry clenched teeth he whispered his intentions. "If you don't get away from us I will shoot you in the head. Now, that I see you up close, I doubt anyone will care."

David Boos stepped up behind Paul Short and tried to end the moment of police brutality. "He ain't worth it Paul. Let him go. He's just one of the crazies."

Paul Short removed the gun from the man's head and stepped back. "You need to go on, now."

The man was still not finished, even if it meant severe bodily harm. "I'll take you to him for five hundred dollars."

Helga was dressed and standing at the door of the room. She had given her sexual lessons she acquired during a lifetime of world travel, practice and experience. Helga was hoping to change her life and she knew Rebecca Coolie was her ticket back to the status she held at one time. With Helga's knowledge and connections and Rebecca's body and willingness to please, there were no limits to what they could accomplish. Rebecca would be used again, but at least next time there was a good chance she would be compensated properly for her talents and services.

Helga smiled at Rebecca. "Please consider my offer as a partnership. I promise you riches beyond your wildest dreams." She turned to Jason. "I know you will not stand in her way if she chooses my business proposition. Good evening to you both."

Rebecca had only responded to Helga's sexual advances. At first it was to please Jason, but as Helga began her magic, Rebecca was more than a willing captivated subject. She had not talked at all during Helga's stay in the room. When the door closed and Helga was gone, Rebecca looked at Jason with her eyes wide open. It was time for Rebecca "Milkduds" Coolie to express herself.

"Holy shit, Jason. What the hell's goin' on? Did she put a spell on me, or hypnotize me? I couldn't stop her or say "no". Did she drug me or somethin'? I ain't never felt like this in my life. I don't know if it's good or bad. It feels good, but I gotta strange feelin' it ain't good at all. What just happened here and what was she talkin' about. Me and her bein' partners and bein' rich? This place is too creepy for me. Let's go, please."

Jason knew how she felt. "I don't know. It's always like that here. They live in another world than the rest of us. Sometimes I think I'd like to be part of it, but it is hard to understand and it scares me, too."

"You want to be like them? Why?"

Jason knew what he wanted to say. "Even with their odd

ways they have more than us. They are better than us. They know more and have done more. We are the weak and they are the strong. They are great teachers but no one will listen to them. People are afraid."

Rebecca was shocked at Jason's deep and profound thoughts. "No shit, people are afraid. People are always afraid of freaks. I just had the most wonderful things done to me in that bed and I'm still scared as hell. There is something wrong with her. Even the ones that are gone, you said they all had something wrong with them. I want to go home. I'd rather face your mama than climb back in that bed with that woman. My head's all messed up. I gotta get out of here. I love ya. But if you're not gonna leave I might just have to go on without ya."

Rebecca had never spoken to him that way. Jason knew she was too scared to stay. "We'll leave in the morning. I'll tell Helga."

Rebecca was please at his response. She was happy to change the subject. "Let's take a shower together and go get something to eat. I'm starvin'."

CHAPTER FOUR

The sun was going down as Mary C. sat alone in a strap bottom lawn chair on Miss Carolyn's front porch. Miss Carolyn was inside the house. Mary C. was dressed for one of her vintage nights on the town. She would still turn heads as she entered any room. As usual, her skirt was tight and short with a blouse just fitted enough to show off her round and firm breasts. There was no doubt she was braless as her nipples became visible each time the temperature would change. There was a good possibility there was a man at Jacksonville Beach who just might get lucky.

Mary C. did not like the fact that Miss Carolyn's new truck was not parked in front of the house. Miss Carolyn came out onto the porch and handed Mary C. a glass of cold sweet iced-tea. "Here, darlin'. I hope it ain't too sweet for ya."

Mary C. took the glass and smiled. "I don't think iced-tea can be too sweet, do you?"

"No, I guess you're right about that. I do love my sweet tea. You look so beautiful all dressed up. You have always been one of our true Mayport beauties. I don't know why, but Mayport has had its fair share of beautiful women. I think it must be from drinkin' the sulfur water."

Mary C. wrinkled her nose. "I don't know about those things, Miss Carolyn. I don't feel so pretty like I used to. Miss Carolyn looked toward the frame of Mary C.'s new house. "It's startin' to take shape over there. We'll be neighbors soon. Are ya excited? I know I am."

Mary C. was never really excited about things, but she loved Miss Carolyn and had to respond in the correct manner. "Yes, ma'am. I really think I am."

"Well, you should be. You'll be starting a new chapter in your exciting life. And if ya ain't, I'm excited enough for both of us." Miss Carolyn could read Mary C.'s face and she wanted to help her. "What is it, darlin'? Why are we sittin' here?"

Mary C. looked into Miss Carolyn's eyes. "Am I that easy to read? I never thought I was that easy."

Miss Carolyn smiled. "Maybe it's just me. I think I know things sometimes I shouldn't."

Mary C. did not respond but she wanted to say, *Me, too.* She knew how Miss Carolyn felt. Mary C.'s visit was two-fold. "I'm not sure where to start."

Miss Carolyn smiled her biggest smile so far that day. "You want to know if a woman like you can walk with Jesus." Mary C.'s eyed widened as Miss Carolyn continued. "I say, 'yes', you can, if you want to. Everybody has choices as they grow. Sometimes we make mistakes, but don't learn from 'em. Most of us didn't choose what we were in the beginning. We had to take what we was dealt. Mamas and daddies make us what we are at first. Some folks remained locked into that first teachin' and never question or expand the information they have. Others break away and find new ways of thinkin'. Some good, some bad, but always different from the beginning." Miss Carolyn reached out and touched Mary C.'s hand. "A person can start a new life any minute of the day. It's making the choice to change that seems to stand in the way. We are creatures of habit, good and bad. Habits are very hard to break. That's why they call 'em habits." Miss Carolyn smiled. "I do talk too much, don't I?"

Mary C. was listening to every word. "No ma'am. You don't." Mary C. put her head down. "I have committed the

deepest of sins. My insides are black. My blood is cold and
I have a rock for a heart. I don't know how or if I could
change all that."

Tears filled Miss Carolyn's eyes. Her hands trembled as
she reached out and touched Mary C.'s hand again. "Oh,
you sweet child. Jesus will take away the darkness, warm
your blood again and soften your heart. You just have to let
him in."

Mary C. still had the second reason for being there. She
was compelled to ask her question. "Miss Carolyn, are you
all right?"

Miss Carolyn's eyes opened wide. "Why do you ask,
darlin'? Does it appear to be somethin' wrong?"

Mary C. wasn't sure what to say but she tried. "Is your
husband good to you? Does he treat you good?"

Miss Carolyn smiled. "You don't like him drivin' the
truck, do ya?"

Mary C. bowed her head and smiled. "No ma'am I don't,
but it's your truck, not mine."

"To be honest with you, I worry every time he drives any
vehicle I have. He's a very careless man."

Mary C. had to ask another question. "Folks call him a
bad man. Is he mean to you?"

Miss Carolyn shook her head. "I've heard that talk, too. I
do know he'll fight if need be, but he never looks for a fight. I
have to say he is not abusive or what I call mean to me. He
has never hurt me or the boys. He has always been respectful,
but just selfish and absent. George comes first with George.
I've pretty much raised the children on my own. He's out
shrimping all the time yet we usually have very little money.
If I didn't have my job at Strickland's, I don't know how we
would live. I feel bad about not being here with the boys at
night, but they're big enough to understand about me workin'.
Willy's fifteen now and Rob's ten. Willy's becomin' a pretty
good young man and Rob has this free spirit that I just love. I
will never break his spirit or let anyone else break it."

Mary C. was not sure if she got an answer, but she had no more questions at that time. She did love the way Miss Carolyn talked. Then the oddest thing happened. Mary C. saw three humming birds flying around Miss Carolyn's head. They were all three hovering with their wings moving a hundred miles an hour. Mary C. was shocked at the sight.

"Oh, Miss Carolyn. You've got three little humming birds flying around you. Oh my God. I haven't seen a humming bird in years. I think I've only seen two in my entire life. Mary C. was even more surprised when Miss Carolyn did not move her head to disturb the three strange intruders. The humming birds remained in their positions. All three little creatures seemed to be looking directly into Mary C.'s eyes. She actually found herself looking back at the three visitors.

Miss Carolyn broke the humming bird trance. "These are my Ruby-throated friends. They visit me every day."

Mary C. could not believe her ears. "You see humming birds every day? I never heard of anybody seein' humming birds every day."

"Well, I do. It's a real blessin' to have these beautiful creatures want to spend time with me. A real blessin'."

Mary C. had more. "This is crazy." With that comment the three little birds disappeared. Mary C.'s eyes opened wide as if she had said something wrong. Miss Carolyn smiled.

"I guess they don't like the word crazy."

"I'm so sorry. I didn't mean to scare them off."

Miss Carolyn laughed. "It wasn't you or the word crazy. They never stay too long. Just hello and then good-bye. They want me to know they're always here for me."

Mary C. had questions. "How long have they been here? I never see any around."

Miss Carolyn took a deep breath. "I don't ever recall them not being here or anywhere for that matter. I see humming birds every day of my life, always have."

The information was too much for Mary C. to absorb. "Humming birds have visited you everyday of your life?

Miss Carolyn nodded. "As far back as I can remember."

"Have you told anyone else about this?"

"Only if the birds show up when I'm talkin' to someone and they mention them." Miss Carolyn smiled as a memory flashed in her head. "They visited me one time when I was talkin' to John on his front porch years ago. They surprised him at first the way they stayed there with me, but when they flew away he had the typical John King response."

Mary C. shook her head. "What did he say?"

"He said, 'You know Carolyn, the Timucuan Indians protected the humming birds because they believed it was the way their departed loved ones were letting them know they were still around and keeping an eye out for them'."

Mary C. had to smile. "That sounds like John, alright."

Miss Carolyn smiled. "I loved his, or I should say the Timucuan explanation for the humming birds being with us. I found out the Timucuans believed the humming birds were the spirits of great warriors. They also carried love and desire to those willing to accept it. I would like to think it is true that they are here to keep an eye out for us. They do look you right in the eyes."

Mary C. did not respond, but she knew exactly what Miss Carolyn was referring to. She felt the three little birds were looking directly into her eyes.

Mary C. was not finished with her questions. "You called them Ruby-throats. Is that a type of humming bird?"

"Yes. I'm usually visited by Ruby-throats, but sometimes I do see a Colliope or the one called Anna's. I've only seen one Lucifer in my life. With a name like that, I'm not too sure those are the good ones to have around."

"You know a lot about humming birds. I never thought about 'em that much. Mainly 'cause I never see none."

"I had to find out about 'em, because I think I am one."

Mary C.'s eyes widened and she was locked into continuing the strange but informative conversation.

"What do you mean, you think you're a humming bird?"

"Well, I know I have always had the personality of a humming bird."

Mary C. could not remember when she was so interested in another person's well being. "In what way?"

"Well, you see, very few people ever see a humming bird. They are literally unseen. I have been unseen my entire life. Like the little bird, I have found a great place in the background. When I'm needed I appear from nowhere and I'm gone when my work is done. They have a great deal to offer the world because they look at everything. They stop to see what is around them. Even though their wings are moving so fast, they can still stop and zero in on what is there and what is important. They seem to be great and caring listeners. I'm a great listener. It's easy to be a talker. The real strength is in being a listener." Miss Carolyn smiled that beautiful smile Mary C. loved. "Yes ma'am, I'm quite sure I'm a humming bird."

Mary C. wanted to talk to Miss Carolyn for hours, but the incredible moment they were sharing on the porch ended when the new red truck came rolling into the front yard throwing dust and pine needles into the air. Miss Carolyn looked out into the yard as the truck stopped.

"He is a careless man. No humming birds around when he's here."

Mary C. agreed with the humming birds. She did not like the way she felt when George was around either. Her uneasy feeling came over her as he walked from the truck to the porch. He spoke first to Miss Carolyn.

"I didn't know you would be home this early. I would have picked you up."

Miss Carolyn smiled. "Me and Pat got off at the same time and she was headed this way. She just lives at the end of the road. I figured you'd be workin' on the boat."

He did not look at Mary C. or acknowledge her presence. Perhaps he could feel she didn't like him. Miss Carolyn had to remind him of his manners.

"Mary C. came by to see her house and have some iced tea. You want a glass?"

"I'll get some." He looked at Mary C. "Some gift." He walked into the house.

Miss Margaret's daughters, Susan and Peggy, were both sitting in their Aunt Peggy's living room with Aunt Peggy and her love interest and roommate, Betty. Aunt Peggy was interested in the girl's strange decision to visit her. She knew something was wrong.

She first looked at her namesake. "Peggy, what's goin' on with you two? What are you doin' here?"

Peggy looked at Susan and then back at her Aunt Peggy. "We just had to get away from the house and the store and Mayport. We knew you wouldn't mind."

Aunt Peggy looked at Betty. "Of course we don't mind. You can both stay as long as you want. But, if I know your mama and my sweet sister, she will be looking for you to come home soon."

Susan wanted to respond. "I don't think she'll care. Not for a while, anyway."

Aunt Peggy needed more information. "You two must understand my worry and concern over this out of the blue situation. I really don't want to press you, because I can see something is very wrong, but on the other hand, it's tough not to ask questions and expect answers. You have both always felt free to talk to me."

Betty smiled. "Would you girls like me to leave the room so y'all can talk?"

Both girls shook their heads. Peggy responded. "No ma'am. You're family, too."

Peggy's comment touched Betty's heart and her bottom lip quivered. Aunt Peggy reached out and touched Peggy's hand as to say "what a nice thing to say".

Susan joined in. She knew they couldn't tell anyone about the role they played in the brutal killings. She said the other things that were on her mind.

"We're just fed up with that store, and with Mama. Having Margie as a sister is like having a second mother. Mama thinks we're still children and it's driving us crazy. We can't spend our young lives in that store. It's not fair."

Peggy looked at her sister and nodded her head in agreement.

Aunt Peggy understood. "Have you tried to sit down and discuss this with your mother?"

It was Peggy's turn. "She thinks we're still her little girls. You can tell when she's not listening. Besides, I hate Mayport. Margie's obsessed with that oak tree. People are getting hurt and even dying all the time. And it seems a new ghost moves in everyday. It's all driving me crazy."

Aunt Peggy was concerned but she knew her two nieces were not telling her the truth about why they had left home and why they really wanted to stay with her. She would let it go for now, but knew there was much more to their story. Mary C. left Miss Carolyn to an evening with her husband and drove back to Mayport.

It was early evening in Gibsonton, Florida. The Big Top Lounge at the Giant's Motel only had a few customers sitting at the bar and one couple sitting at one of the tables. Beulla was playing the piano, but it was an easy listening tune and not her trademark rock-n-roll number. She had turned her babysitting duties over to Rebecca. She was more than happy to stay in the room until they left the next morning. Helga was tending bar and had only served about ten drinks so far that evening. It was a sad state of affairs when only a year ago the Big Top Lounge was packed by eight o'clock in the evening and had standing room only crowds until the early morning hours.

Helga saw Jason the moment he entered the lounge area. She knew why the beauty Rebecca was not there and she had a bad feeling about his visit. He stepped to the bar and sat down on one of the bar stools. Jason knew he was delivering the news and answers Helga did not want to hear. He decided to just tell her as soon as they had the opportunity to talk. Helga took a beer to a customer at the end of the bar and then stepped to where Jason was sitting. She read his face before he could say a word.

"I really scared her, didn't I? I've been so impatient my entire life. I don't know why I have to come on so strong. But she is worth a fortune. I wish I had more time to really take my time and explain it better. She's a natural pleaser and could make us all rich."

Jason tried to add to Helga's explanation of what had happened. "She scares easy. She's had some bad things happen to her. You're right. It was a little too much for her to take all at once. We're leavin' first thing in the mornin'. We need to get back home."

Helga tried not to show her disappointment. "Well, thanks for saying that, but I know I have run you away and I'm so sorry."

"No. It's really time for us to go. I'm sure we'll see you in the mornin'."

Jason did not look back as he left the lounge. If he had looked back, he would have seen a strange look on Helga's face. It was not a sad or disappointed expression. It was mean and angry.

Mary C. walked up onto Mr. King's front porch as he walked out of the front door. He smiled as he sat down in his rocking chair. "You're home early. I didn't expect you until later."

Mary C. sat next to him. "I've been with Miss Carolyn. Do you know about those hummin' birds flyin' around her all the time?"

Mr. King's eyes lit up like the candles he used when he told his ghost stores to the Mayport children. "She's a protected being. She's more than the rest of us. Miss Carolyn will be an angel when her time comes."

Mary C.'s eyes lit up just like his. "What are you talkin' about? I know somethin's strange. She says she sees hummin' birds everyday. Hell John, I ain't seen but maybe two in my entire life. Who sees 'em everyday?"

"An angel probably sees 'em everyday."

Mary C. had to speak up. "John. Do you believe in everything?"

"I'm not sure what you mean."

Mary C. had a flood of reasons for him to consider. "You live in a haunted house. One of your lady friends is a witch. You speak of God and angels. You have used the carousel. You love magic and the freaks of the world. You know all about voodoo and the black crafts of the islands. You say your house is built over Timucuan Indian burial grounds and a Spanish grave yard. And now hummin' birds. I'm sure there's more, but I'm too tired. I don't know what else to say."

Mr. King smiled at Mary C.'s short list of his beliefs. "Damn, Mary C., I never realized how interesting I was. If you think of anything else please share it with me."

Mary C. had to smile and shake her head. "I was on a roll, huh?"

"Very intense, Mary C. Very intense."

Jason sat on the bed with his hand on Billy's little back. The child was fast asleep. Jason could see Rebecca standing naked at the sink in the small motel bathroom. She was looking into the mirror on the wall over the sink. Her side view and profile were exceptional. Rebecca looked great from any angle. It was getting to the point where Jason could not resist her sexual favors. She knew he was looking at her so Rebecca turned, giving him a full frontal view of her incredible body. Even though he had seen her that way many times, it was still a thrill each and everytime. Jason had no control. He motioned for her to come to him. Without any hesitation, what so ever, Rebecca went to him. Billy was asleep near the pillows so there was plenty of room in the bed for Jason and Rebecca to have sexual relations again.

Rebecca was relieved that the crazy Amazon Woman was

not there with them as she positioned herself on top of her man. It was an erotic sight for Jason as he looked up at Rebecca's huge and firm breasts. She reached down and took Jason's blood filled member into her hand, placing it where they both wanted it to be. Her excitement and unnatural fluid release caused his entry to be quick, smooth and deep with the first push of her full round hips. Jason was her perfect fit. It was more like a rehearsed dance than just sex. She moved her butt cheeks with machine-like strokes.

As Rebecca moved her hips, Jason realized he was far too excited and would not be able to stay with Rebecca as long as he had before. His explosion would be sooner than she was used to. She was familiar with his sounds and movement just before he let go. Rebecca usually never talked during the sexual frenzy they created. It surprised Jason when he heard her voice.

"Tell me right before it happens."

It was an unusual request and he did not understand it, but he would do what she asked. Rebecca pushed down harder, adding to even more heat and friction. Jason could not hold it any longer.

"Now! I can't hold it!"

Jason was surprised when Rebecca pulled away from their deep connection and placed her mouth on his exploding manhood. She did not move away as he continued. Jason thought for a few seconds he might actually pass out from the physical strain and intensity. He became dizzy as his blood rushed to protect his sensitive areas. Jason realized he had survived Rebecca's surprise oral attack when she raised her head from between his legs and smiled.

"I wanted to surprise you with something different. I hope it felt good."

Jason blew air from his mouth, hoping to clear his head. He loved it. It turned him into a three question man.

"Who the hell are you? Where ya from? What do you want?"

Rebecca smiled and was pleased with Jason's reaction

and, out of character, humorous questions. She wanted to make it impossible for him to ever leave her. A knock at the door ended their sexual bliss.

Rebecca's heart raced in her beautiful chest as Jason put his pants on and went to the door. She was sure the crazy Amazon Woman had returned. Rebecca was relieved when Jason opened the door and the fat lady Beulla stood there with her big body and big smile.

"I know it's late, but I thought you'd be up. I was hoping I could keep Billy one more night, before y'all leave?"

It took less than a minute for Jason to gather a few essentials for the child and hand him over to Beulla. When Beulla left, Jason took off his pants and returned to Rebecca in the bed.

Mary C. had left Mr. King on his front porch without any satisfaction or answers to her questions. She knew it was his way and he loved people wondering about him. Why was she so drawn to Miss Carolyn? Did the woman out on Mayport Road really have the answers to salvation? Was she protected by the power of the heavens? Can someone really be destined to be an angel? It was all too much for Mary C. to absorb. She took a shower, looked for Hawk in the hot water fog and went to bed prepared for a sleepless night.

Jason woke up with a still naked Rebecca in the bed next to him. She was on her back with the sheet only covering her lower body with her huge perfect breasts pointing at the ceiling. Jason reached over and rubbed her flat stomach for a few seconds and then moved his hand down under the sheet for more early morning exploration. She moaned and was wet instantly. One of Rebecca's many exceptional qualities was her ability to start her body fluids in motion. Jason loved it. Rebecca opened her legs as an invitation for Jason to have his way with her. He loved the way she reacted to him. She had been in a deep sleep and yet she was ready for whatever he wanted. Rebecca "Milkduds" Coolie was almost too good to be true.

Mary C. woke up to the aroma of coffee in the air. She knew Mr. King was up and probably sitting on the porch with a hot cup in his hand. She was surprised when she realized her night was filled with a deep sleep with no interruptions. Mary C. felt refreshed and rested.

Rebecca had only allowed Jason to satisfy her for a few minutes before she began to please him. Her sexual magic was rough, hard and explosive. There was nothing gentle about Rebecca when it came to sexual contact. She was even more excited knowing they were leaving the Giant's Motel that morning.

Mary C. walked out onto the front porch wrapped in her white terry cloth robe. She was even pretty in the mornings. Not everyone is pretty in the morning.

"Well, you sure hit the hay early last night. I thought you were gettin' ready to go out and then I realized you were out alright."

"I know it. I was just so tired for some reason. Once my head hit that pillow I was gone."

"You needed the rest. Thinkin' and askin' questions can flat tire ya out."

"Okay, okay. I get it."

The two friends both smiled and sipped their coffee at the same time.

Jason left Rebecca in the room. He was going to say good-bye to Big Bob and then go get Billy from Beulla. He knew Rebecca was eager to get on the road even if it meant the hardship of facing his mother in Mayport. Rebecca was scared of Mary C. Big Bob was manning the front registration desk. He looked up as Jason approached him.

"Hey partner. What can I do for you this glorious morning?'

Jason had to smile at Big Bob's usual happy attitude. "We're gonna go back home this mornin'. I wanted to thank you for all you have done for me and mine."

"Jason, you and yours are family here. You will always

be welcome. Beulla's gonna be sick about y'all leaving. She loves taking care of Billy. The ol' girl should have had ten kids of her own. She would have been a great mother. But it was not in the cards for the fat lady in the circus."

Jason nodded. "She's been great with Billy. He's gonna miss her, too."

Rebecca's heart jumped when the lock on the door to the room clicked and the door opened. She was excited that Jason had returned and they would be leaving. She moved to the door to greet him. Her excitement turned to fear when she saw two men entering the room. They both grabbed her by her arms. As she screamed and tried to pull away, she felt a cloth cover her nose and mouth. She lost her breath and when she tried to breathe a strange odor filled her nose and burned her throat and lungs. Rebecca's struggle was for only a few seconds but she did hear Helga's voice before an ether induced dream took Rebecca away.

"If you put one mark on this incredible child, you will not lay with me again as long as you both breathe."

Jason told a teary eyed Beulla good-bye and walked out of her room with this son, Billy, in his arms. He walked past the lounge but for some reason he did not look for Helga. He had already told her his plans to leave. As he approached his room he was surprised when the door to his room was open. Jason knew something was wrong when he walked into the room. He could feel it. He moved slowly when the strange feeling came over him. He called for Rebecca, but he knew she was not going to answer him. There was a sheet of paper on the bed. Jason picked it up. It was a note from Helga.

I'm sorry Jason, but I need more time with her. Once she understands, she'll be pleased to be with me. I will protect her. She's my last chance to be free and take my proper place in this world. You will never find us, so go home. Thank you for bringing her to me. It was meant to be. Helga.

Jason, still holding Billy, ran to the front office where Big Bob was still standing behind the front registration desk. Big Bob smiled.

"Morning. Y'all getting ready to head out?"

Jason's voice made Big Bob realize something was wrong. "Rebecca's gone? Helga took her?"

Big Bob was not sure if Jason said what he thought he said. "What? You think Helga did what?"

"She took Rebecca. She asked Rebecca to go away with her, but she wouldn't go. Now, she's gone. Helga took her."

Big Bob had questions. "When did all this happen?"

"It had to be minutes ago. I left her in the room to go get Billy and when I returned, she was gone."

"She must be somewhere around here. Maybe she's in the lounge having breakfast. Let me hold Billy and you go find her."

Jason looked into Big Bob's eyes. "No. She's gone." Jason handed Big Bob the note.

Big Bob held it up and read it to himself. He took a deep breath and shook his head. "I was hoping this desperate nature eating at Helga would pass, but I can see now it was much deeper and serious than we thought. I'm so sorry to bring this on you, but go home, son. You will never find her unless Helga brings her back to you. Let's pray she comes to her senses and does just that."

Mary C. had a strange feeling come over her. She turned to Mr. King. "Jason and Billy are comin' home.'

Mr. King smiled. "Very intense, Mary C. Very intense."

CHAPTER FIVE

It was Jason and Billy's first night back in Mayport from their more than eventful stay at the Giant's Motel. Jason had taken Big Bob's advice and returned home, hoping Helga would release Rebecca. For some reason he knew Rebecca could take care of herself. Jason told Mary C. and Mr. King that Rebecca had decided not to come back with him. She wanted to start a new life on her own. Mary C. had smiled and said, "That girl oughta fit right in with those crazy circus people. She's got some freak in her, too. You're better off without her."

Jason did not like his mother's crude words about Rebecca but he kept his feelings and sexual visions to himself and did not mention Rebecca again. No one else did either. He already missed Rebecca "Milkduds" Coolie, but not enough to gather a search party. Jason was just like his mother. He compartmentalized his feelings and moved on. He was sad he did not have a chance to try and see his old friend, Tom Green. Jason also knew Tom would not have been easy to find.

The sun had gone down but there was still that light that remained just before dark. It was Jason's favorite time of the day. He sat on the steps of Mr. King's porch. Mr. King sat in a rocking chair on the porch above him. Mary C. walked out of the front door holding her grandson, Billy, in her arms.

Mary C. broke the silence. "What a nice breeze out here."

Jason stood up and turned to his mother. "You won't enjoy it too long. Mosquito truck's comin'."

The porch threesome looked down the street to see the mosquito control truck headed in their direction, followed by a thick white fog and what looked like every child living in Mayport. The mosquito truck was like the Pied Piper to the children of the small fishing village. The heavy white smoke coming from the pipe on the back of the truck filled the air with a poison to kill the million mosquitoes breeding and feeding in the Mayport wetlands.

The local children ran behind the truck and would be covered and invisible as long as they stayed in the thick white and toxic fog. Mary C. walked back into the house carrying Billy with her.

Mr. King and Jason remained on the porch as the truck and army of children approached the front of the house. Mr. King wanted to share his thoughts about the fog from the mosquito truck.

"I've always wondered, if that fog is poison and kills mosquitoes, can it be good for those children to run behind that truck. Some of 'em put their faces right up to that pipe as the fog comes out. That's pure poison going right up their nose. And I'm surprised somebody ain't been run over by that truck or another car. You can't see 'em in that fog. I'll bet that poor driver hates comin' down here the way the children act so crazy."

Jason looked back at the front door. "Mama, keep Billy in the house and close that door."

Mr. King smiled as Mary C. closed the front door so the fog would not enter the ghost house. Jason looked back to the street where the mosquito truck was passing directly in front of them. The driver was going very slowly for fear of hurting one of the running and excited children. The driver nodded to Jason. As Jason acknowledged the driver's gesture, Mr. King's eyes fell on a sight he did not want to see.

The Croom twins, Chuck and Buck, came walking out of

the thick white fog as if they were part of the poison. They were too old and too big compared to the other children. They did not fit with the other small children running behind the mosquito truck. While the other children were running, yelling and laughing, the Croom twins were pushing, tripping and laughing at the pain and discomfort they were inflicting on the unsuspecting little ones.

Mr. King hated the twins and his heart raced in his chest at the sight of them. He looked over at his damaged car and hated them even more. Mr. King saw one little girl crying because she had skinned her knee. He did not recognize her but he knew how she had gotten injured.

As Mr. King watched the evil twins, he was shocked when one of them tripped their little, but older brother, Pee Wee. The runt of a child did not know who tripped him as he fell to the hard road. The back left tire on the mosquito truck did not run over him but Pee Wee did receive a rubber burn on his arm. Mr. King would not contain his disdain for the sadistic siblings. He left the porch on a rescue mission. Mr. King planned to save the Mayport children from more bodily harm at the hands of the double demons. He did not know one twin from the other and he did not care. Mr. King's strong right hand grabbed Chuck by his shirt and shoulder and pushed him to the ground in front of the house. Jason watched the action in amazement.

Mr. King then turned and grabbed Buck by the nape of the neck and threw him in the direction of where his brother had landed. Both boys remained on the ground as Mr. King stepped to them. His face was fire-engine red. He liked the thought of scaring and man-handling the young brothers. Anger filled Mr. King's hardened face.

"I can't just sit here and watch you two heathens cause the death of another child, especially your own brother. What's wrong with you two, anyway?"

Jason watched the two boys. They did not try to get up off the ground. It was strange to Jason that they did not seem to care or be afraid at all. It was almost like they enjoyed causing someone to be so mad at them. They were bathing in the moment.

Mr. King had more to say. "You two stay right here until that truck moves on. Y'all too big to be pushin' those little ones around."

Buck remained on the ground but responded. "You too big to be pushin' us around, ain't ya?"

Mr. King was out of control with anger. He grabbed Buck, lifting him off of the ground and held him close to his face. Jason jumped up to be sure Mr. King was not going to injure the child. The child's feet were off of the ground as Mr. King held him up.

"You be sure and tell your daddy about this. I'd like to have another discussion with him about you two little butt wipes." He put Buck down and released him.

It was Chuck's turn to have his say. He remained on the ground. "We don't have to tell our daddy nothin'. You can tell 'im if you want. We don't care." Chuck looked at Mr. King's car. "Nice car."

Mr. King was at his limit with the two seeds from hell. He drew back his fist as if he was going to hit another man. Mary C.'s voice stopped him from his aggressive action. She was standing on the porch.

"John, stop!"

Mr. King opened his clenched fist and moved away from the boys as the mosquito truck turned onto the road between Miss Margaret's store and Mr. King's house. He knew the boys would probably catch up with the truck, but he felt he had done the right thing. He walked back up to the porch and did not talk to the twins again. The boys stood up and stared with four evil eyes directly into Mr. King's soul. Jason did not like what he saw in their eyes. Mr. King did not like the boys being so brave and disrespectful with their evil stare.

"You two need to stop eye-ballin' me. Y'all don't scare nobody. Y'all just bullies and got no friends."

Both boys turned away from Mr. King and looked at

Jason. Chuck used a strange voice.

"Come, she come."

Buck responded. "What letter she come bye?"

Chuck looked at Jason. "CB."

Both boys yelled at the same time. "Crazy Boy." They ran to catch up with the mosquito truck.

Jason turned to Mr. King. He was going to say something but Mary C. took over the moment.

"I told you to be careful of those two, John. I know they deserve what you did, but I don't think they'll ever forget it. And that could be big trouble for you."

Mr. King took a deep breath. "That's fine with me. I won't forget either."

Jason still wanted to add his thoughts. "I'm not sure what's goin' on with those two, but they are creepy boys. Somethin's wrong behind their eyes. It's more than a darkness.

Mary C. could not contain her thoughts. "That's right. Somethin's bad wrong with their eyes. I said that to John when they acted so ugly the other day."

Mr. King had a strange calmness about him. His face was no longer red with anger.

"I don't know why those two boys get to me like that. I've always been nice to 'em and I guess their meanness just rubs me the wrong way. I've seen some bad children around here, but these two are more than just bad. I hate what they did to my car." Mr. King looked at Jason. "It sure is nice to be home, ain't it?" Mary C. joined them on the porch with Billy in her arms. She was more than just happy to have her two boys with her. The fact that Rebecca Coolie had not returned only added even more to her unusual happiness.

Mr. King could see it in Mary C.'s eyes and actions. He had to admit, he was happy to see the two boys as well. They were his family, too. Mary C. sat down with Billy and opened up a can of worms.

"Well, you two, what are we gonna do with Miss Stark's necklace?"

They both turned and looked at Mary C. after her out of the clear blue question. If either one had the answer she did not give them a chance to express it. "John wants to give it to a museum." She looked at Mr. King. "Right, John?"

He did not like her tone. "I did say it is a piece of history and perhaps that would be the right thing to do with it."

Mary C. added to the sarcastic tone he did not like. "And with all the ghosts, angels, witches and damn hummin' birds, we're all obliged to be sure we do the right thing?"

Mr. King was surprised at the way Mary C. was talking. He knew he had to stand his ground. "I have considered other options, but doing the right things keeps creeping back into my mind. Perhaps doing the right thing is not an option for you."

Mary C. did not like the sarcasm Mr. King had sent in her direction. Jason had no idea what his mother was talking about, but he knew she was the cause of the uncomfortable feelings on the porch.

"What's wrong, Mama? Why ya talkin' to Mr. King like that?"

Mary C. was not rational at all. "That's right. You men stick together. And what do you want to do with the necklace, give it back to your big tittied whore?"

Jason looked at his mother with more fire in his eyes than she had ever seen before. "If you don't stop actin' like this, I'll throw it in the river." He put his head down so he would not continue to stare with his mother. "I don't care what you do with it."

They were all silent for a few seconds. Before Mary C. could continue, the sound of a truck motor filled the heavy air. They all three turned toward the noise and saw a rusty green truck headed their way. The truck was moving at a high speed and the driver was blowing the horn over and over again in an attempt to let folks know he was coming and to clear the way.

As the truck seemed to fly by Mr. King's house they could see the driver was Joe Croom. They could also see two men in the flatbed of the truck. One of the men was holding someone wrapped in a green army blanket. It only took a few seconds for the truck to be around the corner past Monty's Marina and out of sight.

Two more cars went speeding by the house with another truck stopping in front of the porch. Mr. Al Leek rolled the driver's side window down and yelled up to the foursome.

"They're takin' Pee Wee to the hospital. The mosquito truck ran over him and he's busted up pretty bad. We know his legs are broken, but there could be more damage."

Mr. King left his chair and walked down the steps to stand by Mr. Leek's car. John King was sick to his stomach. He could not control his rage.

"Damn it, Al! I should have done somethin'. I knew the two freaks were gonna take it out on that little one. I'll be damned if they didn't do just that. I should have made 'em go home. Hell, I should have taken 'em home and talked to their daddy. I hate this, Al. I could have prevented this."

Mary C. joined her friend. "You can't blame yourself, John."

His face was beet red. "They left here and went to hurt that little one. I made 'em mad and those two devils punished him for it. This is too much." He turned away and walked back onto the porch. He looked back at Jason as he entered the house.

"Your mama was right. Those two were tainted when they came out of their mother."

CHAPTER SIX

Big Joe Croom was up early. He had to go shrimping that morning and make some money. He would visit his son Pee Wee in the hospital later that evening when he returned. Big Joe took a drink from a bottle of Jack Daniels whiskey. The warm liquid ran down his throat like children drink kool-aid. It was the nectar of the working man and his breakfast of champions. With Pee Wee in the hospital Big Joe decided to make the twins go shrimping with him. They would work on the boat and he would not have to worry about them getting into trouble. He knew it would not be easy, making them get out of bed so early. They hated going on the shrimp boat. Big Joe had taken them a few times when they were younger but he had to spend too much time keeping them from getting hurt, so he stopped taking them. Pee Wee was usually his extra deck hand. Big Joe knew Mr. King was right about the boys. They were going to do something they would all regret. He would give Mayport a day without his strange sons. He stood at their bedroom door.

"You boys get up. You're both goin' with me today. I can't trust y'all. I gotta make some changes 'round here and it starts right now. Don't make me come back in here. Get up and get dressed." He left the room and went to the kitchen where he took another drink of the hard liquor. He loved the burning sensation he felt as the brown liquid touched his tongue and moved on down his throat.

Big Joe Croom was surprised when Chuck did as he requested and got up and out of bed. Buck took a little longer but he did finally get up. Big Joe had a plan.

"You boys wear somethin' warm. It'll be cool on the way out the jetties."

Chuck was more awake than Buck. "Why we gotta go? We don't wanna go."

The Jack Daniels gave Big Joe his reply. "I don't care if you want to or not. You two are gonna start workin' on the boat with me. You won't behave when I leave you on your own. You skip school if I don't walk ya to the class. You're both dumb as a door knob. Nobody wants y'all around. Pee Wee can't go with me, now. I figure you two will be my deck hands and you can start workin' to pay your way." Both boys stared at their father with that evil eyed look that had become their trade-mark. Big Joe did not like it at all.

"If you think that stupid look scares me, you need to think again. I'm sick and tired of all this bull-shit trouble that seems to follow you two around. I can't trust y'all so you'll stay with me from now on. When ya turn eighteen, y'all can hit the open road with my blessin'. Until then, get dressed."

The twins were silent as their father had one more comment. "Your brother's all busted up in the hospital and you two don't really seem to care at all. Some folks think you are the reason he's there. God, I hope that ain't true." Big Joe lowered his head and then looked back up at the twins. "Now, y'all can help me pay these doctor bills. Get dressed and don't make me tell you again."

Big Joe left the room and walked back into the kitchen. He took another swig of the "golden nectar of the working man." He was a much stronger man when the hard liquor was warming his huge body. He stepped to the twin's bedroom door. He could not believe that both boys had gotten back into their beds as a gesture of grave defiance.

The two boys should have realized their father was a

different man when he walked with Jacks Daniels. Big Joe smiled and nodded his head as to say, *Okay boys, you made the wrong choice here this morning.*

Big Joe unbuckled his two inch wide belt and pulled it out of the belt loops on his pants. Both boys had the bed covers pulled up over their faces and heads. The top of Chuck's head was all Big Joe could see. He stepped to Chuck's bed first and hit the boy on the top of his head with the belt. When the leather slapped against Chuck's head it sounded like someone had hit a puddle of water with the flat end of an oar. Chuck yelled and sat straight up in the bed as the belt slapped him on his bare shoulder. He yelled again and saw the angry look on his father's face. The third swing of the belt connected with Chuck's lower back. It felt like the sting of a wasp as Chuck fell to the bedroom floor and crawled across the floor to find a moment of safety against the wall.

Buck was up, out of his bed and on his feet with a look of shock and horror on his freckled filled face. Big Joe turned to Buck. The flare in Big Joe's eyes told Buck he too would soon feel the burn of his father's belt. He ran to stand with his brother. It was as if they could join forces and have more strength if they stood together.

The rage and alcohol had Big Joe's face blood red. The twins had seen him drunk but never in such a state of anger. This was different. The twins had a rare feeling of not being in control. Big Joe talked through clenched teeth. His words were not slurred by the liquor. They were clear and with conviction.

"You boys get dressed and get in the truck. If I walk out to the truck and either one of you ain't there, ya won't be able to walk for a week. If ya run, I will spend the rest of my life huntin' ya down. Do y'all understand?" Neither boy responded. Big Joe took a deep breath. "I need to hear a 'yes sir' from both of ya. And I need it, now." He stepped toward them with the belt folded double in his huge hand.

"Yes, sir."

"Yes, sir."

When Big Joe Croom opened the driver's side door, the twins were not sitting in the cab of the truck. His blood boiled at first but when he saw them sitting in the back flatbed he got behind the wheel and started the engine. He knew the twins were trying to be defiant by not being inside the truck, but it did not matter. They were going with him and he did not care if they sat with him or not. The two boys had mean looks on their faces. Chuck was mad because he had been beaten and Buck had escaped the burn of the belt. It was as if their father was too drunk and had forgotten to beat them both. They usually shared everything. Chuck's loyalty to his brother had its limits. He wanted Buck to be in pain like he was. It was only fair.

The shrimp boat *Miss Stella* left Al Leek's dock with Big Joe Croom at the wheel. His deck hand, Kevin Brown, was preparing for the first drag while Chuck and Buck sat together on the stern. They were mad as hell, but Buck was not quite as mad as Chuck, or as sore.

The Miss *Stella* moved past the Big Jetty rocks and out into the open Atlantic Ocean, Even though he was full of hard liquor, Joe Croom operated his boat perfectly. Many alcoholics are able to work and perform properly. Some even better than if they were sober.

Miss Margaret was sleeping in that morning. She had not allowed herself very much sleep in the week after she participated in the killings of the drifters. For some reason, she did not dream about that awful day or the humiliation and fear she felt while she was being raped. Her mind and body needed the peaceful sleep. Sofia opened the store that morning so her exhausted mother could get some rest. The bell on the door sounded and Sofia turned to greet her first customer. It was Robert Fussell. She smiled and gave the traditional greeting. "Good morning, Mr. Fussell, may I help you with something? How are you feeling?"

Mr. Fussell had not expected the young and beautiful,

Sofia, to be in the store that morning. He hesitated with his answer at first but recovered. "Good morning. I'm doin' just fine. I came by to thank your mother for her kindness. I stopped by John's but there's no one at home. Just the ghosts I guess."

Sofia loved that ghost talk. "I'll bet they're running wild without Mr. King there. Mother's taking the morning off, but I'll be sure and tell her you came in. Is there something I can help you with?"

A million things Sofia could do for him ran through his head in a split second. His mouth went dry and his heart raced at the possibilities. It was difficult for any man not to want a moment with the likes of Sofia. But, Robert Fussell was a true gentleman and his thoughts would stay in this head.

"I think I'd like a cold strawberry Nehi to start the day and make my tongue red." He wasn't sure why he said that. His face got as red as his tongue would soon be, but Sofia smiled and that was all that mattered.

He pulled an ice cold bottle of the red colored drink from the drink box and walked to the counter to pay. Sofia moved behind the cash register so she could conduct the business at hand. "You can open it at the box or I can open it here." She held up the silver bottle opener that was tied to a white string on the counter. "Would you like me to open it for you?"

Mr. Fussell handed her the wet bottle. "That would be fine. Thanks."

Sofia smiled and opened the bottle. She smiled and handed it back to Mr. Fussell. She knew he was older, but thought perhaps he was thirty or so. He was no doubt younger than most of the people she met. He was clean-cut in appearance. He was a fireman. Sofia did not want to lose his company.

"So you're a fireman?"

Mr. Fussell was surprised the beauty had questioned him. He hesitated, but like before recovered. "Yes, ma'am. Ten years now. I started when I was eighteen, right out of high school. Never wanted to do anything else."

He was younger than Sofia thought. She wanted the conversation to continue. "How's your lip doing? It's still swollen. Is it very painful?"

"Only if you make me laugh."

Sofia smiled. "Well, you don't have to worry about that. I'm never too funny."

Mr. Fussell smiled, too. "Me neither."

The bell on the front door of the store rang and they both turned to see who was interrupting their conversation. Sofia's ice blue eyes lit up, her heart raced in her beautiful chest and her mouth went dry when Jason walked into the store. Mr. Fussell had never met Jason, but he had heard stories about Mary C.'s son. He had no idea of Jason's connection and past history with Sofia.

Jason smiled. "Good mornin', Sofia." He looked at Mr. Fussell and nodded.

Now, it was Sofia's turn to hesitate and then recover. "Good morning, Jason. Just getting back home? How's Billy? Is he doing good?" Sofia was a nervous three question woman.

Jason continued to smile. "Got back yesterday. Billy's fine. He's gettin' big."

Mr. Fussell knew he had lost Sofia's attention and the surprise conversation was over and done. He picked up his bottle of strawberry Nehi and looked at Sofia.

"Thanks Sofia. Don't forget to tell your mother how much I appreciate her."

Sofia smiled as he walked toward the door. "I won't forget, Mr. Fussell. Thank you."

When Sofia turned back to Jason he was nose to nose with her beautiful face. She tried to step back away from him but he put his strong arms around her small waist and pulled her body to his. The kiss came quickly. It was hard and passionate. Her body seemed to fuse itself to his. Sofia did not want to kiss him at all, but the fit was too good. The fit had always been too good. She returned the passion Jason began. It was where she was supposed to be. It was as if she had never been without him. In only a few steps they were in the back stockroom of the store. She did not want to be there, but there she was. Sofia saw Jason's tanned and muscular chest. She had no idea when he took his shirt off. She looked down to see that her blouse was unbuttoned exposing her firm, round, snow white breasts. She did not remember that happening either. Jason opened her blouse and pushed his chest against hers. The heat was unnatural when their skin met. Sofia pushed her breasts toward him. Once again, a perfect fit. They were like a single ball of fire. Sofia did not care that he had been gone, no doubt been with other women and would probably leave her again. She did love Jason. You cannot help who you fall in love with.

Jason reached down and rubbed Sofia between her legs over her pants. The single stroke made her shiver. She felt her pants drop to the floor. There was another single stroke of Jason's hand on the outside of her panties. She wanted to touch herself, but waited on Jason's next touch. She stepped out of her pants on the floor as she felt Jason pulling her panties down with, what seemed to be, one motion. Sofia stepped out of her panties and kicked them and her pants to the side.

Jason was totally naked. She knew he had undressed himself. Sofia was still wearing the unbuttoned blouse. She was braless from the beginning. Jason grabbed a blanket from a shelf and threw it on the floor. The blanket had not reached the floor when he took Sofia down on it. Sofia was on her back waiting for Jason's body to pin her to the floor. He stood over her and looked at her body from her beautiful face to her perfect feet. Jason knelt down at her feet. Her heavy breathing, her loving eyes and her tempting lips overpowered him. He reached down and grabbed both her ankles with both his hands. Sofia felt her body fluids run down the inside of her thighs. With one pull from Jason's hands her long perfect legs were wide open; wider than they had ever been before. She was looking in Jason's eyes and then they were gone as he put his face and head between her opened legs. The passion and heat Sofia experienced when Jason's tongue entered her body was not something anyone ever expects until it happens again at another time. Jason locked onto both her legs with this forearms and pulled her body even closer. Her knees bent and she tried to open her legs even wider. Jason drove his face and tongue as deep as he could as Sofia pushed so he could reach his goal. Her stomach muscles were contracting every few seconds as the flow of her sexual fluids pumped out of her like some one had pulled down on the lever of a big lipped water pump. She could not control the flow or the contractions.

Sofia thought Jason would stop his oral assault and want her to please him, but he did not. He wanted her to remember him and want him everyday. She reached down to lift his head and end the muscle contractions. She pulled his hair but he did not release his hold. Sofia felt it coming from her toes. She knew she had never felt this way before. She tried not to scream as the explosion began. It took every muscle in her body to remain on the floor. When it came, Jason released her and with one push he drove his manhood deep into her body. His mouth covered hers as the kiss muffled her sexual noises. At first it was too sensitive when he entered her. She straightened out her bent legs and actually wanted to crawl away from her beloved Jason. He would not let her go. He made her fight through the sensitivity. Once it passed, she wanted more. Sofia was in another dimension of sexual pleasure and wanted to stay with Jason until they both burst into flames.

She heard the muffled sound of the bell ringing on the front door of the store. For a moment, she did not care. Sofia mentally returned to the stockroom when Jason pulled away from her and stood up. His quick departure from their physical union startled her as she tried to focus on the task at hand; finding her clothes and getting dressed. The bell on the door had only sounded once so Sofia knew there was a customer waiting for someone to assist them. Her heart dropped into her still flexing stomach when Jason kissed her on the lips, told her he loved her and ran out the back door of the stockroom, holding his shoes and shirt in his hands.

Jason was fully dressed and walking up to Mr. King's front porch in a matter of seconds. He stepped up onto the front steps. He looked back at the store and wanted to touch Sofia again.

Sofia was not sure how she looked when she entered the front of the store from the stockroom. She heard voices from behind one of the shelves, but did not see who was in the store with her. The voices stopped and there was silence for only a few sounds. Sofia stepped behind the front counter waiting for the customers to appear. For some reason a strange and uneasy feeling came over her when she realized the Croom twins were her new customers.

They were big boys. She had not seen them in awhile and was shocked by how they had grown. She had always been kind to them, but they were cute little boys. Sofia was looking at two young men with no remnants of ever being little boys. She knew it was the twins right away, but their appearance had changed drastically. They were no longer those cute little boys. They were ugly young men with faces of pain and torment. She smiled and tried to hide her nervous and strange feelings.

"Good morning, gentlemen, may I help you with something?" Sofia's voice cracked and she cleared her throat. "You two have sure grown up since I saw you last. I almost didn't recognize you."

The twins were like wild dogs and they sensed Sofia's fear and hesitation. They approached her and stood side by side in front of the counter. Chuck spoke first.

"You're Sofia, the prettiest one, ain't ya?" His eyes were

black and Sofia did not like his voice. It did not seem to fit him. She thought perhaps it was a voice he created to scare others. Sofia did not respond. It was Buck's turn to add his two cents to the uncomfortable situation.

"Where's Margie?"

Sofia remembered how Margie told her about helping the twins when they had the Joe Jumpers stuck in them at the sand hill. The twins only remembered looking down Margie's opened blouse at her bare breasts and nipples. Even though Sofia was the prettiest, Margie would always be their favorite. They had also watched Margie perform her sexual ritual on the limb of the oak tree, endearing her even more to the sexually perverted young twins.

Sofia's voice cracked again. "She's visiting some friends. I haven't seen her in a few days. I'll tell her I saw you two. I know she'll be pleased."

It was obvious neither boy was listening too her. Sofia was hoping Jason would walk back into the store so she would not be alone with the odd siblings. Her pounding heart jumped when the bell on the front door rang. It did not matter to Sofia who was coming in as long as she did not have to be there alone with the twins. Her fears and worries were erased when she saw Jason walk through the front door. How did he know she needed him? How could he always be her hero? How could she live without him? Sofia did love Jason and she was a three question woman again.

"Good morning. May I help you with something?"

Jason did not smile as he looked at the twins. He felt the tension and evil in the air. He responded to Sofia's greeting but watched the boys.

"I just came by to say hey and let you know I was back. I was hoping we could do something tonight, if you wanted."

Each twin grabbed a handful of penny candy and dropped them on the counter. Sofia counted the variety of pieces. The boys did not look at Jason, but he continued his stare toward them. He did not like the boys and he liked them being there with Sofia even less.

Sofia finished counting the pieces of penny candy. "That's fifty cents all together."

Each boy put a quarter on the counter to pay for the candy. Sofia put all the candy in one bag. Chuck took the bag and they both walked to the front door. Jason knew they were uncomfortable with his constant stare in their direction. The bell on the door rang when Chuck pulled it open. Chuck turned back to return Jason's stare. His voice sounded as if it was coming from someplace else.

"Come she come."

Sofia looked at Jason. Jason looked at Chuck. Sofia knew the word game, but this was too strange. Chuck turned away from his stare and looked at this brother.

"Come she come."

Buck had the proper response again. "What letter she come bye?"

Chuck gave Jason a pure evil smile. "DM."

Both boys stood at the door. Buck held it open. They both smiled at Jason and yelled, "Dead Mama" as they ran and the door slammed.

Sofia was so relieved they were gone and so excited to see her real life hero and one true love. She walked from behind the counter and threw her arms around him.

"How did you know I needed you? What made you come back so soon? Don't you think they're creepy boys?" Sofia was sticking to her dramatic personality. Jason had to smile.

"I came back because I was hoping we could do something tonight. I want to be with you. I miss you and I love you."

It was a crazy love and Sofia knew it, but she could not change her feelings for Jason. She was not sure if there would be more disappointments because of the way she felt, but that didn't matter at the moment. Everyone needs a hero and Jason was hers. Sofia also wanted his head between her legs again and it did not matter when or where. She was addicted to Jason's oral abilities and his willingness to please her.

Sofia kissed Jason. He drove his tongue deep into her mouth as a reminder of his talents. She felt her stomach muscles contract. When the kiss ended, Sofia's panties were wet again.

"I would love to do something tonight." She wanted to add, "As long as your head is between my legs," but Sofia was too much of a lady to speak in such a vulgar manner. She had more. "What happened to those twin boys? It's like they've been sick or something and the illness caused them to change permanently. They really scare me. I hated being alone with them. Thank you for coming back when you did."

Jason smiled and had his opinion about Chuck and Buck.

"I think I agree with Mama. She thinks they were born with tainted blood. She even said they had mildew in it."

Sofia made a face. "What a strange thing to say. I never heard of anyone having mildew in their blood. Is that possible?"

Jason thought he understood the concept his mother was trying to relate when it came to the boys affliction. "I think she just means they were born to do bad things. Like it was in their blood and they had no choice. While others are making excuses for the way they act and look, Mama says they were born to be evil and they have been since the air touched 'em. Most folks probably don't believe that, but Mama does."

Sofia had to add to the creepy conversation. "Well, your mother usually has the answer to most things. Knowing her as we all do, it's hard not to put credence into what she thinks and says. All I know is that something is terribly wrong with those two boys and the thought of mildew in their blood sounds as reasonable as anything else. I don't like being scared when they are around. They were just cute little boys and now they look and act like they are of the devil. How could such an awful thing happen?"

Jason was glad Sofia stopped talking. He was going to take her back to the storeroom and she would have gone willingly, but the bell on the door rang again as another Mayport citizen entered the store. Sofia's eyes widened once again when she saw her Aunt Peggy walk through the door. Sofia's beautiful face lit up when she saw her aunt. Peggy's face lit up when she saw Jason. She had memory flashes of the times he had taken her to the sexual mountain and thrown her off, lit up her mind's eye. She would always have those stomach butterflies when she was near Jason. She had fond memories about him. He could have her any time he wanted.

Jason was always excited when he saw Peggy, too. He liked the way she looked. She was thick and hard and a tad over weight, but the extra pounds were distributed into her butt, breasts and full lips; all the proper places. Jason had a few mind flashes of his own and remembered how Peggy walked around her house wearing only her panties and bra. He wanted to see that exciting vision again. Peggy was more than willing to fulfill his fantasies.

Sofia greeted her aunt first. "Aunt Peggy, what a nice surprise." She stepped to Peggy and hugged her. "What are you doing out this way?"

Peggy nodded to Jason. "Hey, Jason. Long time no see."

Jason nodded at her, too. "It sure has. You doin' alright?"

"I'm good. I've been workin' a lot out at the Hideaway. I've been there 'bout a year, now. Tips from the tables been pretty steady and I'm on the bar on the weekends. I'd like to be on the bar full-time but that's a highly coveted position. I'd probably have to sleep with somebody for that job. I just ain't sure who yet. But, when I find out, I'll be bar tendin' full-time."

Sofia bowed her beautiful head after her aunt's crass statement. Jason had to smile at Peggy's raw but realistic spin on her life as she saw it.

"I'm sure you will. I didn't know you were out there. I need to get over there for dinner one night."

"Be sure to ask for my table if I'm on the floor."

Jason and Peggy both knew their generic conversation was over. Peggy looked at Sofia.

"You all right, sweetie?"

Sofia wasn't sure why that question came from her aunt. She was cautious with her answer. "Yes, I'm fine. How are you?"

"I'm good, but I'll be even better if I can find out why Susan and Peggy are plannin' to live with me for awhile. I came here to see your mother, but perhaps you can shed a little light on this strange and most disturbing situation I'm facin'." Sofia's stomach went sour as her Aunt Peggy continued. "I ain't gettin' jack shit from your two sisters, pardon my French so I thought I'd see what's goin' on." When Aunt Peggy opened her eyes wide and looked at Sofia, she thought she saw an actual question mark on Aunt Peggy's facial expression. Aunt Peggy waited on Sofia to respond.

Sofia felt bad about not answering her aunt's inquiry. She did not want to be disrespectful, but she also did not want to betray the others. She looked at Jason. He understood her dilemma. Once again, he came to her rescue.

"Things been crazy as usual around here, Peggy. I was just discussing it with Sofia and it seems Miss Margaret wants to be the one who gives out the details if anyone is interested. I'm sure that's why Sofia and the others don't have much to say. You know how Miss Margaret is."

Aunt Peggy knew exactly how her sister was. She looked at Sofia. "I'm sorry for putting this pressure on you. I'm goin' to see your mother, right now. I need to know what's goin' on." She touched Sofia's pretty face. "You sweet thing." Then she turned back to Jason. "Don't forget to ask for my table if you come out to the restaurant." Aunt Peggy was out the door and on her way to see her sister, Miss Margaret.

A return trip to the back storeroom was on both their minds. Even as risky as it was Sofia did not care. She looked into Jason's eyes and read his carnal mind. She reached out and took his hand as the bell on the door rang again. Three separate customers entered the store. Sofia let go of his hand.

Jason smiled and leaned in close to her ear. "I'll come get you at seven."

She pressed her nose to his cheek. "I'll come to you."

CHAPTER SEVEN

Aunt Peggy drove up to Miss Margaret's. Her older sister was sitting in a rocking chair on the front porch. She had a shawl around her shoulders. It was obvious Miss Margaret was still in her night gown. Aunt Peggy had never seen her sister looking so pitiful. She got out of her car and walked to the steps of the porch.

"If you've got some highly contagious disease please tell me to run for my life." Miss Margaret did not smile at her little sister's observation, but she did respond.

"That bad, huh?"

Aunt Peggy stepped up into the porch. "Yes. That bad." She sat down in the chair next to her sister. "What the hell is goin' on around here? I ain't seen so many sad people in my entire life and they're all related to me. I came to you for an explanation. Nobody else seems to have the answers I need. Now, no silly games here, Miss Margaret. What has driven your wonderful children away from you and into my living room and for God's sake why are you sitting here like an old woman waiting to cross over?"

Miss Margaret had to smile at her sister's dramatic but accurate observation. "Are the girl's alright?"

"I guess. They seem fine physically, but mentally they're wrecks. I could even see it on Sofia's face when I was at the store. What's wrong with all y'all?"

Miss Margaret took a deep breath. "You saw Sofia?" Aunt Peggy nodded. "What did Sofia say to you?"

"Nothing, just like the other two. So you're it. It's your turn. No one has betrayed you. The big secret has been protected. Now, let me in on whatever is goin' on. I can keep a secret better than all of y'all."

Miss Margaret did not want to, but she had to smile again at her younger sister's way of presenting her case. Her smile left her face as she blew air from her mouth.

"If I explain this to you, you cannot tell anyone, not even Betty. The more folks who know the more likely someone will tell it. You know that's true."

"I do know that, but I can't promise not to tell Betty. She's like family and she cares about the girls and you. You'll just have to trust my judgment on that."

One more deep breath and Miss Margaret was ready. "You heard about the drifters who got killed last week?" Aunt Peggy nodded her head. "Well, we killed 'em."

Aunt Peggy's lips went dry. "Who killed 'em?"

"We did. Me and the girls. We killed 'em."

Aunt Peggy still wasn't sure. "You and the girls killed all those people?"

Miss Margaret nodded. "And Mary C."

Aunt Peggy's eyes widened. "And Mary C.?"

"Yes. And don't blame her. I think it was my idea, but I'm not sure about that. I asked for a gun and we all decided to kill 'em all."

Aunt Peggy could not believe what her sister was telling her. She was lost for words but Miss Margaret had plenty.

"They violated us and they had to die. They were horrible things. I don't even think they were real people." The "not real people" comment disturbed Aunt Peggy but she did not respond as her sister continued. "I'm sorry about the woman, but that can't be undone. I'm not sorry we did it. I'm just sorry I took the girls with me. That's the hardest part for me to live with. I ruined their innocence. What kind of mother does such a thing?"

Aunt Peggy was in mild shock over what she was told. It was difficult to pull her thoughts together. Not in a hundred years would she have thought such a thing would have happened to her family. She knew it was one of those secrets a person must take to the grave.

"There was a woman, too?"

"Yes. Perhaps she did not deserve to die, but she was with them."

Peggy took a deep breath. "Tell me how something like this happened."

Mr. John King stood next to the hospital bed where Pee Wee Croom lay with his left leg in a full cast and his right leg wrapped and elevated in traction. Pee Wee looked pitiful as he tried to remain still and not move the wire and cable apparatus holding his leg above him. He forced a smile when he saw Mr. King. Such an effort from the young victim knotted Mr. King's stomach and he fought back the manly tears welling up in his eyes. Pee Wee's pain and discomfort were so obvious that Mr. King said a silent prayer in his mind and asked God to take the boy's pain and put it into his body so the child could have some relief. It was a sincere prayer. It was a prayer many adults have said when a loved one was in pain. It was also a prayer that is never answered.

"Hey, little buddy. You doin' alright?"

"Yes, sir. It hurts when I move. It's hard to keep from movin' but if I hold still, I can handle it."

Mr. King smiled. "I know you can." Mr. King looked up at the metal and wires holding Pee Wee's leg in the air. "I'm so sorry about this."

"It ain't your fault, Mr. King. You saved me the first time. I just got hurt that's all. I gotta be more careful next time. No more chasin' the mosquito truck for me."

Mr. King loved the young man who talked like an adult and blamed no one for his pain. He sat and talked to Pee Wee for two hours. They even laughed a few times. Mr. King left when the doctor came to adjust the traction wires.

Mr. King did not want to see his young friend in such pain.

Miss Margaret had told the story of the sexual and mental abuse they had endured at the hands of the strangers. Aunt Peggy listened to her older sister's description of the abusive ordeal and the justified brutal retaliation. Miss Margaret told her how Susan was the only one who the nasty drifters did not torture in some way, but Susan did kill as revenge for the others. Tears rolled down Aunt Peggy's checks as the unforgiveable and life changing acts were explained. Aunt Peggy hated the drifters and she had never seen them. She was glad they were dead. She understood the need for belly burning secrecy. She hugged her sister again.

"I'll keep your secret. Let the girls stay with me for awhile. What about Margie?"

Miss Margaret shook her head. "I don't know where she is. She just left."

Margie walked up to the Band Shell stage as the members of the band were setting up their instruments for the evening performance. She had heard about the evening dances at the Band Shell but had never been there before. Margie liked to dance. She just didn't get many chances to do so. She was hoping that would change soon. All five men working on the stage stopped when Margie walked to the stage. She liked that. Margie smiled as her attire made the introduction.

"Hello gentlemen. You must be the band."

The band member closest to he nodded. "Yes ma'am we are definitely the band. And who might you be?"

"I might just be, Margie."

"Well, 'I might just be Margie', what can I do for ya?"

The other band members had stopped their activity to look at the beautiful, sexy and alone young woman.

Margie could see the band members were not as young as they looked from a distance. She knew they were older than the crowd they would be playing for later that night.

"I was wondering what time do you start playing? I

would like to come back and listen. And your name?"

"They call me, Bodach. This is my band." He pointed to the other men on the stage. "This mass of hair, chains, tattoos and muscles behind me are the Night Shadows." The other four men nodded to Margie with want in all eight eyes.

Margie returned the nod and then directed her attention to the band leader. "Thank you. It was very nice to meet you, Bodach. I've never met a band before, or a Bodach. Is there a hidden meaning behind Bodach?"

The band leader smiled. "There are always hidden meanings behind names. The fun part is finding out what it is."

Margie smiled, turned and walked away. She made sure not to turn back and allow her new friend to enjoy the view as she left. Margie looked as good leaving as she did coming. It was a gift.

Peggy drove away from her sister's house in her Volkswagen. She knew what she had been told was true but it was still a hard reality to swallow. She would not question Peggy or Susan anymore and was not sure if she was going to tell her roommate, Betty. She would have to make that decision when the time came.

Margie was standing near the Ferris Wheel on the Board Walk eating a mustard coated corn dog when she heard the music at the Band Shell begin. The sounds of the drums and bass guitar filled the air first letting the beach goers know the evening of music and dance had officially begun and was in full force. Margie was excited as the sound of the boogie woogie music was carried on the beach wind. She slid the last bite of her corn dog off the stick with her perfect white teeth and tossed the clean stick into a trash can. She was drawn to the music and she had already met the band.

Miss Margaret pulled open the screen door at the front of the store, but the main door was locked. She looked through the glass and did not see Sofia in the front of the store. She knocked but there was still no movement inside. Miss

Margaret thought perhaps Sofia had locked the door so she could go to the bathroom without a customer coming in. They all did that from time to time when needed.

Sofia was in the back stockroom with her pants off and her long perfect legs opened wide. She could only see the top of Jason's head again. It was her new favorite position. She touched his hair as he pushed his tongue deeper and pleasured her to her limits. For Sofia to lock the front door and let herself go was affirmation to her new oral sexual addiction. She laughed and moaned at the same time when Jason pushed against her and moved his head back and forth. It was too much for Sofia as her sexual fluids covered Jason's mouth and chin. He moved away and wiped off his face with his hand. Sofia was spent. She rolled over onto her stomach exposing the perfect curves of her back, butt and legs. Jason got on his knees, grabbed her waist with both hands and pulled her butt to him. She was on her knees facing away from him. When Jason entered her it was that one deep push he loved. Sofia moaned and tried to pull away because of the sensitivity but Jason held her in the position he wanted. She had no choice but to fight through the discomfort. It was a small concession when she knew what he would do for her later. Sofia was addicted. Jason was out the back door.

Miss Margaret had been waiting about ten minutes and she was getting worried about Sofia. She stood up as she heard the click of the lock latch on the door. Miss Margaret was standing there when Sofia opened the door. She was surprised to see her mother standing there.

"Mother, you scared me!"

"Scared you? I was going to go home and find my key. I was scared something had happened to you. At first I figured you where in the bathroom. Are you alright?"

Sofia felt her face fill with blood. She lied. "Yes ma'am. I was in the bathroom. My stomach has been upset for about an hour now."

"You dear thing. We're all so stressed, it's a wonder we're not all sick."

"I'm fine, now. Honest."

Miss Margaret did love her Sofia. "Well, why don't you go on home and relax. I need to do some paperwork here. You are such a dear for allowing me to get some rest."

Sofia was excited to be able to leave. "Did you talk to Aunt Peggy?"

Miss Margaret nodded. "Yes. She knows everything."

Aunt Peggy drove her Volkswagen into her front yard. Betty was sitting in a lawn chair, wearing a bikini and sunning. Her suntan lotion covered her body. Betty did have a great body and very little was covered up. Aunt Peggy loved her men but for some reason she loved kissing Betty's full lips and sucking on her nipples.

Aunt Peggy got out of the car and sat down next to her roommate. "That's my favorite suit ya got on there, Miss Betty."

Betty smiled. "That's why I have it on, Miss Peggy."

Betty could take or leave the men they encountered. She really just wanted Peggy, but she did not interfere when she wanted a man. Betty was not going to do anything to hurt the relationship she had with Peggy. Peggy had made it very clear that there would be times when she needed a man. Betty also knew they were together more and more without a man. Peggy and her sister Susan walked out of the house. Susan looked at Betty and was shocked at how small the bathing suit was. Peggy smiled at the look on Susan's face. She whispered to her sister. "She always wears stuff like that. She walks around the house naked, too. So get ready for that. Don't faint when she does. I've seen her do it twice. If we stay here, you'll see."

Both girls walked slowly down the steps and into the yard where Aunt Peggy and Betty were sitting. Susan had no words as she scanned Betty's body. Peggy looked at her aunt. "Did you talk to Mama?"

All eyes turned to Aunt Peggy. "I did. She told me everything. I understand it all, now. It is truly a family secret and will be that forever." She looked directly at Betty. "We will not discuss the matter again."

Margie did not move to the stage when she first made her way through the crowd of spectators and dancers. She stood in the back ground and watched the others. As her head rotated from side to side scanning the dance floor, she could not help but realize how many eyes were watching her, both men and women. She liked that. Most people would.

The crowd at the Band Shell was a mixture of locals and townies. Townies were anyone living on the west side of the Florida Intracoastal Waterway. The beach dwellers called it "the ditch". Townies were on the other side of the ditch. Some were dressed to kill, while others should have been killed for what they were wearing. The folks who had been on the beach all day were barefoot and still wearing their bathing suits. It was always a good thing when one of the young females danced in her bathing suit, but not the fat boys. The majority of the female dancers came dressed in the latest styles. Short-shorts, pedal pushers, tight short skirts, and shirts tied at the waist were all part of the Band Shell fashion.

Margie was perfect and a true cut above most of the others. Perhaps three or four other young women were on her level. She felt excited and confident as eyes moved with her. Margie saw a group of young women dancing in front of the stage. They had no partners and were dancing alone and facing the band. Margie joined them.

Sofia walked up the steps to her front porch and unlocked the front door to the house. There was movement to the right side of the porch. Her heart jumped at first as she turned her head not knowing what or who might be there. Her heart raced even more when she saw Jason coming toward her.

Sofia turned to face him as he grabbed her in his arms.

He pushed the door open with his strong arms and lifted her up off her feet. He held the door open with his foot, carried her inside and closed the door with the same foot. Sofia felt like she was floating as Jason carried her up the stairs and into her bedroom. She thought perhaps it was just one of her better dreams. Sofia's first hint that it was all happening was when Jason pulled off her pants and literally ripped her panties off. Then she was positive when she saw the top of Jason's head placed strategically for her oral pleasure.

Margie was dancing to the music but for the band. She didn't need a partner. The members of the band could not stop watching her. Bodach was the lead singer and sang a number of songs directly to Margie. It was as if he had already staked his claim on her. He had a hard look about him. His hair was shoulder length and his face was scarred from a complexion problem from his youth. A number of other scars on his face were from being a man.

The other band members had the same hard look about them as their leader and they started working their individual magic on the other young women dancing near the stage. They were all marking their territory for later in the night when the music stopped and the Cold Duck was being consumed. The members of the band had discovered that the Spanish Fly pills dissolved faster in the Cold Duck than any other beverage. It was their system of assuring the young women they took back to their hotel rooms would stay and were willing to perform for them. They were definitely Night Shadows of the lowest moral fiber.

Sofia was on fire. She had to crawl away from Jason's oral attack and beg him to stop. Once again he turned her over and pulled her butt toward him as he took her from behind. Sofia was prepared for him this time and she fought through the sensitivity, allowing Jason to enter her.

The Night Shadows were taking a break. Margie watched Bodach with her peripheral vision as he stepped down from the stage to stand with her. She did not want to seem

interested. She was looking away from him when he stepped
up next to her.

"Damn woman, I can't stop watchin' you. Please don't
dance up front there during our second set. I couldn't take it.
Go dance in a corner somewhere."

Marie turned to face Bodach. "You're running me off?"

"Only to keep me from lookin' at you all night. I'm
supposed to be lookin' at all the women near the stage, but I
can't if you're up there."

She looked into his eyes. He did not smile. "You're
serious."

"Yes ma'am. There ain't one other woman like you in
this crowd. These young, local groupies come to see us play
all the time. It's always good for our egos and we do have
some real fun now and then, but no one like you. I'm just
scared you won't be here when the dance over."

True or false, Margie loved his words. "I probably won't
be here if you make me dance in the corner."

Bodach took a deep breath. "Will you promise to stay
and have a drink with me?"

Margie smiled. "You'll find me in that corner over
there." She motioned to the right side of the stage.

Bodach smiled and kissed her on the lips. She did not
pull away until their lips touched. He smiled. "I'll meet you
in the corner."

Jason was lying on his back in Sofia's bed. It was her
turn to pleasure him with her perfect full lips. Her long
blonde hair covered his stomach, thighs and privates. He
could not see her but he knew what she was doing. Jason
also knew Sofia was a novice when it came to oral pleasure,
but he also knew she would get better. He allowed her lesson
to continue until she wanted to stop. He would pull her away
before he exploded. Jason had experienced oral sex experts
in his many sexual encounters. He was in love with Sofia.
She didn't have to be an expert.

Margie was dancing in her corner as if she was still

standing in front of the stage. She was watching Bodach as the men in the crowd watched her. The music began and the words "walkin' the dog" came from Bodach as he thrust his hips and pelvic area forward toward the crowd. The crowd at the Band Shell erupted into a boogie, woogie, dirty dancing frenzy. The dancing couples seemed to be stuck to each other as if someone had melted them together. The young women were pushing their butts back toward the young men standing behind them. The young men were more than willing to push their pelvic area against the ladies' butts. They were all "walkin' the dog".

Margie watched the dancers as they moved near her. The young men standing behind the women sent sexual memory flashes slamming into her brain. That was her favorite sexual position. Margie wanted someone behind her. She went up on her toes as if she had a partner. Her panties were wet. She could feel it.

Jason pulled Sofia up toward him and had her sit across his body. She moaned and lost her breath when he entered her again. Jason reached up and took her perfect breasts in his hands. He had instructions as he squeezed them.

"You move. You make it go deeper."

Sofia had lost all the inhibitions she ever had. She followed Jason's command and they both would scream with pleasure before she stopped moving.

The Night Shadow's took their second break. They would play one more set before midnight for the wild beach crowd. Margie watched Bodach walk down the steps of the stage and look in her direction as a young woman stopped him. She was not a teenager, probably in her late twenties. They talked for a few seconds then she kissed him on the lips and moved away. He walked to where Margie was standing.

"One of your groupies?"

Bodach smiled and looked back at the young woman as he answered. "Oh, that's 'No Panty Annie'. She's more than a groupie. She's an institution. She does love her music."

Margie could not believe what she was just told. "You call her 'No Panty Annie'?"

"We call her Annie to her face, but she knows we call her that."

Margie shook her head. "She really doesn't wear any panties?"

"Well, sometimes she doesn't, but if she does, they hit the floor pretty quick, if you know what I mean."

"I think I do."

Bodach was very nonchalant about his relationship with "No Panty Annie". Hey, she's a real trooper, that one. She'll do anything for ya."

Margie was disgusted. "I'm sure she will. With a name like that, I'm sure she will."

"No, I mean it. She's a great person. She's a free spirit when it comes to droppin' her panties but she's a good woman. I'd trust her over a lot of people I know. When "No Panty Annie" tells ya somethin', you can take it to the bank."

Margie did not like the conversation about the free spirited "No Panty Annie". She knew she was going to like it even less when she saw "No Panty Annie" walking in their direction.

Margie turned away as Bodach turned to his female friend. "Hey Annie, I want you to meet someone." Annie looked at Margie as she turned around. "This is Margie. Margie this is Annie."

"No Panty Annie" stuck her hand out to shake with Margie. "I'm pleased to meet you, Margie. Bodach said you were the most beautiful woman here tonight and I had to see for myself. He has a tendency to exaggerate now and then." She smiled at Margie. "But not this time. You are beautiful."

Margie was surprised at her comment. It took her a few seconds to remember her manners and respond. "Thank you. That's very kind of you to say."

"No Panty Annie" smiled and held Margie's hand. "You're welcome."

Bodach smiled and looked at Margie. "You still gonna be here after this last set?"

Margie pulled her hand away from "No Panty Annie's" grip. "I told you I'd be here in the corner. I always keep my word."

"No Panty Annie's" eyes widened. "Me, too. You're only as good as your word."

Margie did not dance like she had before with "No Panty Annie" standing with her. Margie was not going to talk to her new acquaintance unless she had to, but "No Panty Annie" had never met a stranger.

"You a local woman, Margie?"

Margie nodded her head. "Yes, I live in Mayport."

"That's where the ferry boat crosses the river, huh? I think I have some relatives over there. They say they're Minorcans. I think that's what they call 'em.

Margie knew about Minorcans. "There's a lot of Minorcans in Mayport."

"No Panty Annie" had her thoughts. "Are they poor? People that fish all the time seem poor. My relatives never seemed to have anything."

"It's a hard life. I see it everyday."

"What do you want to do, Margie?"

Margie was not sure she wanted to become friendly with a woman called "No Panty Annie". "Let's just say I just stepped out into the world and leave it at that."

"No Panty Annie" smiled. "I like that. You're a woman of mystery. No more questions from me."

They both turned to watch the band. "No Panty Annie" had no more questions but she did have a comment.

"He's quite taken with you, but you must know that. You're in for a great night if you're interested and can handle it."

Margie was intrigued by "No Panty Annie's" challenge, but did not respond as Bodach's voice blasted out from the microphone. "The midnight hour approaches and the Night

Shadows have more work to do. Thank you for spending your evening with us and we hope to see you again. Good night and be safe." The band ended with the instrumental, Green Onions, one of Mary C.'s favorite songs.

Bodach stepped down from the stage while the band played the last tune. He walked directly to Margie. Margie took a deep breath as the sweaty, wet, long haired, tattooed band leader approached her. As if she knew to get out of his way, "No Panty Annie" moved away from them. He was only a foot away from Margie before he stopped. She thought he was going to kiss her again before he spoke. He didn't.

"I was watching you. I was scared you were gonna leave." He remained inches away from her.

Margie was uncomfortable with his face so close to hers, but she wanted to show him she could handle whatever he presented.

"I told you, I'd be here. Now, what?"

Bodach smiled. "Good question. You hungry?"

It was an unexpected question. Margie stumbled with her answer but got it out. "Sure, I guess so."

"Great. Bodach need food." He took her hand and walked her toward the Board Walk while the band was still playing.

Jason and Sofia lay in her bed. The sheets were wet from sweat and the release of body fluids. Jason liked the fact that Sofia had drained him. He was already looking forward to more moments like that one. Jason knew he had stayed too long and needed to leave. He was going to ask Sofia to get dressed and go have dinner with him somewhere. But Sofia was different. Before he could speak she sat up in bed and made a request.

"Will you put your tongue inside me again?"

Margie sat at a window table at Strickland's Seafood Restaurant. It was located on First Street in Jacksonville Beach with a view of the Atlantic Ocean. Margie's room at the Sand Piper Hotel was only a few blocks away. Bodach had left her at the table to go wash up from his four hours of entertaining the Band Shell crowd. Margie was mentally tired from the stress of leaving home and being out on her own and physically tired from standing around for four hours waiting for Bodach. It was also after midnight. She was not used to being up on the move at such a late hour. She smiled as Bodach walked back to the table and sat down across from her.

Bodach looked even older in the light of the restaurant. She had only really seen him either at a distance or when he was closer and it was dark. His face was rough and drawn with lines from late nights, sleeping all day, booze and drugs. When he smiled Margie could see he was missing the tooth behind his eye-tooth. It wasn't noticeable unless he smiled but it was still gone. A missing tooth very seldom adds to a person's good looks. Margie was having serious second thoughts about her decision to join Bodach. The waitress arrived with a bottle and placed it on the table. Evidently, Bodach had ordered it when he went to clean up.

Margie had never seen a bottle of Cold Duck before. "What's this?"

Bodach took the bottle and twisted off the sealed cap. "This is Cold Duck. It's a very sweet drink. I think you'll like it."

"What a strange name for a drink."

Bodach poured her a wine glass full of the dark liquid and then one for himself. Margie had a problem with wanting others to know she was not weak or scared. She thought about "No Panty Annie's" challenge and took her first drink of Cold Duck. She liked it.

Sofia crawled away from Jason's mouth as she moaned and released her fluids. Jason did not follow her escape as he had done before. He had nothing left to chase her with. Sofia lay motionless as Jason sat up on the edge of the bed. He touched her back and took a deep breath.

"Can we get somethin' to eat, now?"

The fried shrimp dinner at Strickland's was over. One bottle of Cold Duck was empty and the second bottle had very little left in it. Margie was feeling the effects of the sweet elixir, but she still did not want her night to continue with Bodach.

"This has been very nice. I'm not used to being out so late and I'm very tired. Thank you for dinner."

Bodach could see what was happening and was not going to allow this beauty to just walk away after he had planned to spend the night with her.

"Well Margie, you're quite welcome. Perhaps we can do it again sometime."

Margie was relieved at his attitude about her leaving. "You never know what might happen."

Bodach smiled his biggest smile of the night exposing the hole where the tooth used to be. "You sure are right about that. You never know what's comin'"

Bodach poured the last of the cold Duck into both glasses. "One more drink and we'll call it a night." He held his glass up. Margie picked her glass up and touched it to his. It was a toast to one last drink and she would be free. Margie emptied the wine glass with one swallow. She had no idea a dissolved Spanish Fly pill was mixed in the Cold Duck. Bodach was a master at slipping the erratic horse drug into a woman's glass of spirits. It was his twisted way of still being able to attract the young beauties, like when he was younger as well. It had turned into a sick ritual and Margie was the next victim.

Bodach was not his given name. He was obsessed with the thought of being a child of the night. His life style and even the name of his band spoke volumes about his twisted personality. When he read about the shadow type creature called Bodach, he became Bodach that very day. The mystical beast had been known to come in the night and steal the innocence of young people, especially young women. A

Bodach seems to appear in the shadows just before a disaster
and they thrive on the misery of other creatures.

Margie and Bodach were standing on the sidewalk in
front of Strickland's Restaurant. She could hear the waves of
the ocean crashing onto the shore. She could also feel the
effect of the Cold Duck. The salty breeze touched her face.
She could see the Sand Piper Hotel only two blocks away.
She turned to Bodach.

I'm staying right down the street."

He looked toward the hotel. "The Sand Piper?"

"Yes, that's it, the Sand Piper."

He smiled. "That's an interesting choice for a young
lady."

Margie nodded. "I didn't know very much about the area,
but I'll stay the night and do something different tomorrow."
Margie stuck her hand out to Bodach. "Well, thank you
again for a fun evening."

Bodach took her hand and pulled her to him, kissing her
in one motion. Margie allowed the kiss to continue for a few
seconds but did not actually return it. Bodach stepped back
and smiled. He knew he had lost her for the moment but he
also knew it was only a temporary setback. He was a
despicable character. He was Bodach.

"Do you need me to walk you down there? I don't
mind."

Margie shook her head. "No. You've been kind enough.
It's only a block or so. I'll be fine." She turned and left
Bodach standing there. For about a full block she did not
look back. She liked the cool breeze coming off the ocean
and the smell of the salty air. Margie was a little light headed
as the approached the sidewalk in front of the Sand Piper
Hotel. She turned and looked back toward the restaurant
where she had left Bodach. He was gone. Margie was glad.
She turned and entered the downstairs lobby of the hotel.

Margie passed the front desk where the night attendant
was asleep with his head on the counter. He did not move as

she passed by him and walked toward the elevator. There was a sign on the elevator door that read: *Sorry. Please take the stairs.*

Margie shook her head and moved to her left where the door to the stair well was located. Her room was on the third floor so it wasn't as bad as the tenants on the upper floors.

Margie stopped after she reached to door to the second floor. She was a little dizzy and stopped to settle her head. She knew the Cold Duck had really kicked in. Margie felt a sensation between her legs. She rubbed herself to make it go away. It was as if she needed to scratch it away. Her mouth went dry and her heavy heart beat come out of nowhere. Margie wanted to get to her bed and satisfy herself. She wished she was straddling the oak tree. That would ease the itch that was deep inside her.

Margie did not remember climbing the last steps to the third floor, but she was standing at the door of her room. The key fit perfectly and she found herself standing in the room at the Sand Piper Hotel. She turned back to close the door and she was facing Bodach. He was standing as close to her as he did at the Band Shell. He scared her.

"Oh God, you scared me."

He closed and locked the door. "I figured I would. I didn't want to, but it was necessary."

Margie was actually throbbing on the inside. She was hot and wanted her clinging clothes off her body. Bodach recognized her deep breathing as one of the normal reactions to the sex drug he had given her.

Margie knew she was in trouble but her body was boiling inside and she needed something or someone to ease the heat. She tried to resist what was taking place.

"Please go. I don't want you here."

Bodach stepped to her and smiled. The only thing she saw was the gap from the missing tooth. "You'll want me here in just a few more seconds."

Bodach knew the pill had kicked in and Margie was

ready for any object inside her body. He stepped forward and placed his hand against Margie's crotch and rubbed her up and down. She could not move away or resist his touch. She was too dizzy and he was rubbing her in the right spot. She felt her pants and panties fall to the floor and his fingers were touching where she needed to be touched. She was wet and could not stop her stomach muscles from contracting. She knew when Bodach took her blouse off and she was completely naked. She bounced on the bed when he pushed her down and crawled in after her.

CHAPTER EIGHT

The only place open that late at night near Mayport was the Red Barn Bar-B-Q. That was fine with Jason. He was just hungry. Sofia was just hungry for Jason but she did eat more than Jason had ever seen her eat before. He liked that and so did she.

Margie had been tossed around her hotel bed like she was a rag doll for at least an hour. Bodach had been on top of her, underneath her, and behind her. Margie felt pain at certain moments but the pleasure far outweighed the discomfort. She could not stop Bodach from his sexual assault. He could do whatever he wanted. She was helpless. Margie knew she had been an active participant to satisfy the sexual drive raging inside her body. She needed Bodach to scratch her itch but she knew she would never drink Cold Duck again.

It was two o'clock in the morning when Sofia got home. Jason stood on the porch until she unlocked the front door. Sofia could tell her mother was not home and had stayed at the store. She turned and smiled at Jason, took his hand and pulled him into the house. Sofia was different.

Margie woke up. She was lying on her stomach with her left arm hanging off of the hotel bed. She could see the floor next to the bed. Her head throbbed as bad as her other body parts did the night before. She tried to lift her head and realized she had been drooling on the striped mattress under her face. The clean white hotel sheet was gone. Margie forced herself to sit up on the edge of the bed. Her stomach burned, her legs were sore, her lips were dry and chapped and her butt hurt inside and out. As she put her feet on the floor, she saw one of the bed sheets in the corner of the room with drops of blood stains.

Margie was afraid again as she turned to face her abuser. Margie's eyes widened when she realized Bodach was not in the bed with her. Hot liquid from her burning stomach filled her mouth when she saw two of the other band members sleeping in the bed. Bodach had violated her and then shared his spoils with a few friends. He was despicable. Margie was sick.

She hurried and dressed as fast as she could, watching the two Night Shadows, in case they woke up. She was ready to run, dressed or not if they moved. Margie got to the door holding her small bag in her hand and looked back at the two sleeping slime balls. If she stepped a certain way her butt hurt. Margie knew about revenge. She had faced it before. There was no reason to run and hide. The Night Shadows had never seen a woman like her. She slowly placed her little bag on the floor by the door. Margie picked up the dungarees of one of the men and went through the pockets. She found a bag of blue pills and five one hundred dollar bills. With such a first find she went through the pockets of the other pair of pants that were on a chair. She found only two hundred dollars, but she found something better than money to her at the moment. It was a big knife in a leather sheath. The handle was pearl white and the silver blade was divided in the middle forming two separate sharp blades.

Margie had never seen such an instrument of death. The handle fit perfectly in her small hand. She walked to the side of the bed and stood over the sleeping Night Shadows. It was their fault that they had chosen the wrong woman. For some reason she thought of Mary C. and Margie knew she was doing the right thing for herself and any future young woman who might have had the misfortune to dance for the band from hell.

One of the men sensed her presence standing over them and he opened his eyes. "Hey baby, you ain't leavin' are ya? Bodach said for you to stay until he got back."

Without another thought or response, Margie slashed out with the knife, slitting the man's throat wide open from the bottom of his left jaw bone to the bottom of his right jaw bone. It was so easy. It sliced like butter. He grabbed his bloody throat but made little noise. The other man did not move as his evil companion was bleeding to death next to him.

Margie was committed now and she could not stop. The twitching between her legs was gone but now her drive for revenge needed to be scratched. She liked the fact that her first victim saw who was slicing him open. She reached over and shook the other man with her free hand.

"Hey Shadow Man, wake up. I got your breakfast." He moaned, but did not open his eyes. "Hey mister I need you to open your eyes so I can cut your head off." Margie liked that. It seemed appropriate and very truthful.

He opened his eyes. "What did you say?"

The man did not even know he was cut until the blood gushed into his mouth. Margie stood over him until he stopped choking. She moved away from the blood soaked bed and stood near the door. She had to wait for Bodach. Margie thought she would be whole again if she faced the despicable one.

Sofia kissed Jason at her front door. They had not gotten very much sleep. Jason spent most of the night with his head between her legs. His jaw was sore from his effort, but he loved the fact she was addicted. Sofia wore an opened robe exposing her perfect naked body. She wanted more.

"Will I see you later today or tonight?"

"If I can get some sleep. I ain't much good without a few hours sleep."

"Then go get some sleep. You know I love you? I always have."

"Yes, I do know that. I love you, too."

Margie was only waiting about ten minutes when she heard voices in the hall outside the room. She heard a woman's voice and then she recognized Bodach's voice. Margie thought it must be "No Panty Annie" coming to join the sadistic party. She listened and could hear Bodach.

"You go on back. We'll meet ya for breakfast."

"Don't forget me, now,"

"I said go on. We won't forget ya."

Margie could hear "No Panty Annie" walking away down the hall. The knob on the door turned and Bodach walked into the room. It was a small room and he saw the two bloody bodies of his friends as soon as he walked in. Before he could react in any way he felt like someone had put a white hot poker against his throat. He reached up with his right hand and felt his warm blood flowing onto his hand. Margie was standing in front of him out of his reach. He had no final words. Even if he had a few, he could not speak them. Bodach dropped to his knees and then fell forward with his face slamming to the floor. Margie wiped the blade clean on the cloth arm of a chair, put the knife in her little bag and left the room. She was whole again.

The hall and stair well of the hotel were empty that early in the morning. No one was manning the front desk when Margie put her room key on the counter. She hurried out the front door and walked toward the bus station. She wanted to get away from Jacksonville Beach, but did not want to go back to Mayport. She was surprised at how calm she felt after she had so brutally ended the torturous habits of the Night Shadows. She stepped into the bus station and sat down at the food counter. Her heart jumped in her chest when she saw "No Panty Annie" sitting alone at a table. Margie knew she was waiting for Bodach and his henchmen to join her for breakfast. Margie wanted to go tell her to go ahead and order, they won't be joining you, but she decided it would be better to move on before "No Panty Annie" saw her. Margie left the bus station and walked south to the Board Walk. She needed to sit somewhere alone and make a plan for her next move.

Jason walked up to the front of John King's haunted house. Mr. King was sitting in his favorite chair with his morning cup of coffee in his hand. He smiled and shook his head as Jason stepped up onto the porch.

"Good mornin'. How was your night?"

Jason smiled. "You wouldn't believe me."

"Oh, now that's where you're wrong. Nothin' would surprise me when it comes to you and the ladies."

Jason stepped to the front door. "I gotta get some sleep. Mama up yet?"

Mr. King shook his head. "I don't think she slept here either. Last night I was alone with friendly spirits."

Jason stopped. "I hope she's alright."

"I'm sure she is."

Margie sat at a small round table upstairs at the Oasis Bar and Grill in south St. Augustine, Florida. She was a woman on the run. It was early on a Saturday evening and the bar was filling up with locals, and the folks traveling on Florida Highway A1A. The Oasis was a favorite watering hole for everyone, young and old. Most of the time, it was filled with a mixture of lifetime St. Augustine residents, tourists, and bikers, local and on the move. The food was good, the atmosphere was great, the music was loud and the clientele was pure honky tonkers.

Margie had already ordered a glass of sweet tea and special of the day fried grouper fish sandwich that came with fries and coleslaw. She had enough money to last a week or so but she was trying to conserve what she had. She knew she would have to find a way to make some money pretty soon. She had no intentions of returning to Mayport.

It was about eight o'clock when Margie finished her

meal and three glasses of tea. She was walking back to her table from the bathroom and could see that the tables and bar stools were filling up with customers. People were standing against the walls and moving around looking for that empty space or someone to leave. It was going to be a standing room only crowd. There was a four member band setting up in the far corner of the room, preparing to rock the house. As she got back from the bathroom, she saw two young women standing next to her table. She smiled at the tall one with the blond hair. The woman reminded Margie of her little sister, Sofia. No one was as beautiful as Sofia, but the girl's body and hair were similar to Sofia's. Margie had two empty chairs at her table. The tall blonde smiled back at Margie.

"If they're not taken, could we use these two chairs?"

Margie nodded and pushed one of the chairs out from under the table. "I'm alone. Help yourself. If you'd like to sit here that's fine, too. There isn't much room left in here, is there?"

The tall blonde nodded her head. "That's Saturday night at the Oasis."

Both young ladies pulled out the chairs and sat with Margie. They both thanked her and the blonde made the introductions.

"This is my sister Tiff and I'm Susan."

"Pleased to meet y'all, I'm Margie. I have a sister named Susan and you favor my little sister, Sofia." Susan smiled as the waitress returned to the table. Margie paid her tab and the waitress cleaned off the table. Susan knew what she wanted.

"I know you're busy but when you have a moment please bring us each a top shelf Jose Cuervo margarita and be sure it has a shot of Grand Marnier."

The waitress nodded. "I'll be right back."

Susan turned to Margie. "The least we can do is buy you a drink."

Margie had no idea what a margarita was or who Jose Cuervo was for that matter, but she wanted them to think she was worldly and not a Mayport bumpkin. It was one of

Margie's flaws. She worried about what other people thought about her.

The four band members were tuning up and took their places on the small stage. The three top shelf margaritas were delivered to the table. When Margie had the glass placed in front of her she noticed the ring of salt on the rim. She acted like she had seen it before. Susan lifted her glass up first.

"To an evening of dancin' our butts off?" Tiff and Margie lifted their glasses and the toast was complete. Margie's first sip of the tequila mixture was her introduction to Mr. Jose Cuervo one of her new best friends.

The band at the Oasis began the instrumental introduction to the song, "Walkin' the Dog." Margie turned toward the band as the memory flashes of Bodach filled her head. The Night Shadows had played that popular song, too. The lead singer talked while the music played in the background.

"Good evening ladies and gentlemen and welcome to the Oasis. Just one look at us and you'll know why we are the "Missing Links". We ain't pretty boys, but we can burn this mother down." The crowd exploded with whistles and cheers. He waited for the noise to fade. "Thank you. Feel free to sing along, dance or just get drunk with us. We hope to make your evening better than it was before you walked in that door. Ladies and gentlemen, we *are* the Missing Links."

Ask my mama for fifteen cents, see an elephant jump a fence, hi-ho, tippsie toe, she broke her needle, now she can't sew, walkin' the dog...

The place exploded again as the crowd sang the song along with the band. Susan and Tiff were singing and dancing together next to the table. It was easy to see they were sexy young women. Margie liked the wild, colorful and spontaneous atmosphere. She took a moment and looked at the band. It was no doubt the strangest looking group of men she had ever seen. Even before they named the band they were the missing links.

The lead singer was also the lead guitarist. He was a tiny man, probably five feet tall. He wore a black cowboy hat that was too big for his little pea-sized head. The hat covered his entire forehead, ears and his eye brows. His long sleeve powder blue western style shirt had a colorful horse head embroidered on the front and back. It sparkled when the lights hit it. His faded dungarees were frayed at the cuffs and he was barefoot.

One of the backup singers played the harmonica and the tambourine. He was tall with a huge completely bald head. He wore a green and yellow flowered unbuttoned Hawaiian shirt exposing a fat white belly with a silver dollar size naval hole. They had just started playing and the big man was already sweating like a pig. His big forehead and cheeks were glistening with perspiration and drops of sweat dripped off of his chin when he was not playing the mouth organ. The bold man's most outstanding feature was the fact he had only two bottom teeth. Only his two canine teeth remained on his bottom gum line.

The drummer was the youngest member of the Missing Links. He displayed a goatee-beard and mutton chop side-burns. His white round top safari helmet added to his odd appearance.

The fourth member of the band and bass guitar player was by far the most bizarre of them all. He was skeleton skinny with long white hair. He had a small patch of thin hair in the middle of his deep receding hair line that he had allowed to grow so he could comb the patch forward to cover his eyes. He wore a pair of cut off jeans showing his white toothpick legs. His stained white wife-beater style undershirt revealed his wienie arms. His crowning glory was the amount of white hair he had growing on his body. It actually looked like the fur from a baby seal. It covered his shoulders and back. The hair extended out from his chicken chest about three inches. It was obvious why he wore the wife-beater shirt. They were an odd collection of individuals, but they could play.

The Oasis was the place to be and Margie was there. She loved the excitement. She felt she was meant to be in such a place. Margie paid for the second round of margaritas. When they were brought to the table Margie took a big drink and then stood up to dance with her two new friends.

All eyes were on the three dancers. You could look at the band just so long before your eyes needed a break. The three dancing young beauties had become part of the evening entertainment.

The third round of drinks came to the table without them being ordered. They were the compliments of a man sitting at the bar. The waitress pointed him out and he held up his glass as a salute to the three women. Susan raised her glass toward him as a "thank you". He turned away and began talking to the female bartender and her visible four inch cleavage line.

"It never fails. We start dancin', drinks start comin'." Susan looked at Margie. "You really added to the party." Susan looked over toward the bar. "He sent us the drinks so he will have a reason to talk to us later. He'll make his way over here a little later. He wants to act like he's just being friendly from over there, but he thinks we are obligated to at least talk to him."

Tiff wanted to add her thoughts. "He wants somethin' he ain't gonna get." She looked at her sister. "Or maybe he will. You never know."

Susan smiled and looked at Margie. "Tiff is more of a free spirit than most. I like to make a man work a little if he gets me. You know, wine and dine."

Margie nodded as Tiff joined in. "I've made 'em work before, but if I see someone I like why make us both wait when we both know how it's gonna end up? She looked at the man at the bar. "I've always liked older men like him. They know stuff. They don't need directions like they're lost or somethin'. Best sex I ever had was with a fifty year old man I met at the pool. I liked the way he showed me respect before he fuck your brains out."

Susan hit her vulgar sister on her arm. "Stop talkin' like that. You start drinkin' and you become a foul mouthed slut."

Margie's eyes widened as the sisters began a verbal assault on one another. Tiff hit Susan on her arm, too.

"Don't hit me or call me a slut, you tight ass whore."

Margie's eyes widened more as the sisters burst into laughter. Susan laughed even harder when she saw the expression on Margie's face.

"Don't mind us. We're both sluts." Susan shook her head and looked at Tiff. "Yeah, it starts with a few dirty words poppin' out of her mouth and ends up with her pants on the floor somewhere."

Tiff rolled her eyes at her sister's comment, looked toward the band and changed the subject. "Are they the ugliest four men you've ever seen in your life?"

Susan agreed. "I wonder how they were able to find each other."

"Birds of a feather."

Margie's three margaritas with salt and Jose Cuervo had dulled her mind and loosened her lips. "I sure hope I don't have to kill one of 'em."

Her strange and out of place declaration silenced the sisters. They looked at each other and then they both looked at the intoxicated Margie. Tiff had loose lips, too.

"What the hell does that mean?"

Margie had no idea what she had said. "What?"

Tiff looked at Susan and then back at Margie. "You said that you hoped you didn't have to kill a band member. Why would you say that?"

Margie had a puzzled look on her face. "I don't know why I said that. It just came out of my mouth. I guess I'm a slut, too."

The two sisters exploded with laughter again. They all took another drink.

Tiff was still laughing. "Damn, I just said they was ugly. Margie here wants to kill 'em for bein' ugly."

The loud laughter continued and the Missing Links played on, as margarita number four was delivered to their table, once again compliments of the older gentleman at the bar. Tiff was feeling the effects of the potent Cuervo Gold. She left the other two at the table and went to thank their admirer in person.

Susan had seen this type of action before. "Oh no, Tiff's drunk. We might have to save her."

Margie looked toward the bar to see Tiff walk up behind the man and put her arms around his neck, pushing her breasts into his back. Susan had more to say.

"Oh Lord, she's really drunk. She's already touchin' him. That Tiff has always been a toucher. She don't mean nothin' by it, but men take it as an open invitation or somethin'. That's why we go out together, now. If she's out alone and gets drunk, it's open season on Tiffany Jones. But, I do have to say, it's usually her fault. You really can't blame the poor horny men. They're gonna take advantage if they see a weakness or an opening. Tiff will sure open those legs of hers."

Margie was drunk, too and had no control over what was coming out of her mouth. "You two ever doubled up on a man?"

Susan smiled her biggest smile of the night. She was excited and more than willing to tell her double team story.

"Oh my God, yes we did. I ain't never told nobody this story. We did that one time. We was both so drunk. It started with us jokin' around with a friend of the family. He was older and we both had a crush on him when we was growin' up. We both knew he had been with lots of women, but that made him more attractive as we began to learn about boys and then men. Me and Tiff been talkin' about sex since we was in elementary school. He was a Marine and had to go back that next day and me and Tiff ran into him at a beach party."

Susan stopped talking and looked to be sure Tiff was still

at the bar. She was and Susan continued her story.

"We all went back to his apartment and it just happened. I really don't think it was his fault or intentions. Once Tiff got drunk, started talkin' dirty, got naked and suggested we get in his bed, it was wild. He was just what we always expected. He was an expert in bed. It was a great night. He left for the Marines and was dead six weeks later. I'm not sure how he died. I'm sure glad we spend that one night with him."

Margie was sad. "I'm sorry he died."

Susan wasn't listening as she continued her thoughts about her friend. "Tiff was really scared for awhile. She didn't start her period of over a month and a half. I think she started the day we found out he was dead. Weird, huh?"

Tiff was still wrapped around the man at the bar. His left hand was squeezing her butt cheeks. Either Tiff was too drunk to feel his advances or she didn't care that he was touching her. No matter what the reason, Susan went to save her foul mouth slut sister. She left Margie alone at the table as the band took a break.

While Susan was thanking the man at the bar for the drinks and prying Tiff's arms from around his neck, Margie realized her lips and legs were both numb from the tequila. She emptied her fourth glass and as she placed the glass back on the table, the skinny, hairy bass player wearing his stained white wife-beater undershirt was standing next to her table. His forehead and long hair were dripping wet with sweat. His extremely thick white chest hairs looked like a wave going up his neck. The little man was as disgusting as a person could be, but he was attracted to Margie.

"You do know, you're the best lookin' woman in the house tonight, don't ya?"

Margie nodded her beautiful intoxicated head. Her mouth was out of control. "Yes, sir. I do know that. But you need to know that I've already killed three band members and I would hate for you to be number four. So please go away. After three others number four would be easy. I'm a slut but I ain't openin' my legs for you. You look like a wooly booger."

After Margie's slurred insult, she stared at him with a drunk goofy smile. He grinned back at her with a mad and embarrassed smile.

As he walked away, Margie slid her thumb across her throat in a slicing motion. He did not see it. Susan and Tiff returned to the table with a new game plan for the rest of the night. Susan had the details.

"Tiff's new friend over there has a house on the beach. His name is Roland James. He's fifty years old and acts like he's got money up the butt. He invited us all to go see his new place. He says there will be about twenty people there around ten. He also said no strings attached. We can leave if we don't want to stay. I figure with three of us we'll be pretty safe. What do ya say, Margie, you in?"

Margie smiled that goofy smile. "As long as I don't have to kill that wooly booger over there." She pointed at the bass player.

Susan shook her head. "I promise you won't have to kill anybody."

Tiff had another thought for Margie. "But you might have to be a slut."

They all laughed again, including Margie. "I do believe I can handle that."

Roland James stepped up to the table where the ladies were still laughing. They stopped when he smiled.

"You three have really been a great deal of fun over here tonight. I hope you will bring some of that fun and energy to my little get together. I do understand if you don't show, me being a stranger and all, but I can assure that you will be safe and hopefully have a good time. Here's the address and directions from here if you decide to stop by." He held out a small business card. Tiff took it out of his hand. Then Margie took it from Tiff.

"Hell, you can't even see it much less read it."

Roland James looked at Margie. "I haven't had the pleasure of meeting you. I'm Roland."

Margie had that silly smile. "I'm Margie. Wooly booger killer. Are you a wooly booger?" She reached for his shirt as if she wanted to unbutton it and see if he had hair on his chest. He stopped her.

"I'm not sure what that is, but I can assure you I am not one." He looked at Susan. He knew she was the only one in control of her faculties. "I do hope you ladies will come by. I have really enjoyed meeting you three. If you decide not to come perhaps we'll meet again. Hope to see you later."

Roland James left the three young beauties too make the decision. Susan looked at the card he gave them.

"This guy's a damn doctor." She looked at Margie. "Please don't kill him."

Margie nodded. "I just kill band members. I like doctors."

Dr. Roland James' new house was located on State Highway A1A just north of Vilano Beach. The three ladies could hear the music playing when Susan parked her car on the side of the road. The front driveway area was filled with vehicles. It took them about twenty minutes to drive from the Oasis so the effects of some of the early tequila had dissipated. Margie had lost her goofy grin and Tiff would not drop her pants when she walked in the door. Perhaps later but not right away. Susan had never lost her edge. She seemed to have her wits about her at all times. She was a true drinker and survivor.

They crossed the road and walked up to the huge double doors. Tiff rang the door bell. It was a Spanish style mansion surrounded by sand dunes. A beautiful woman dressed in tight white short-shorts opened the door. Her long legs were tan and perfect. Her high-heel shoes made her calf muscles bulge. Her flat stomach was exposed below a six inch cleavage line. She was older than them, but she looked great. It was the look of money.

"Please come in. I'm sure you were invited, but even if not, do come in."

The three young ladies walked past her and looked into an open foyer full of beautiful people. Some were standing and talking. Some were dancing at the end of the open area. The music was coming from a huge stereo system that lined the wall. The three beauties only stood there for a few seconds before Dr. Roland James walked over to greet them.

"Well, I wasn't too sure you would come. Welcome to my home."

Susan was the most alert of the three. "It's beautiful. Thank you for inviting us."

"Thanks for coming. I hope you don't mind the music, I'm quite an Elvis fan."

Tiff had to get here two cents in. "Who don't like Elvis?"

He nodded and smiled. "Exactly. Please help yourself to food and drinks in the next room. The bartender makes a great margarita. I promise you won't be disappointed."

Tiff could not contain her outburst. "Damn, you got your own bartender. That's pretty cool."

"Well, it's just cool for tonight. She's a good friend and she's helping me with my house opening. I probably won't have a private bartender again."

Tiff was not finished. "No man. This is a party house. The bartender will return at a later date. We will, too."

Susan had to rescue her sister. "Let's just try to make it through this evening without breaking anything and perhaps if he ever has a party again, we can be his bartenders."

Dr. James smiled. "That's a deal."

Margie was not as drunk as she had been but her lips had a little too much freedom. "I'm glad there ain't no band. I don't do good when there's a band."

Susan did not want anymore, "I might have to kill somebody", talk from Margie. She joined in quickly. "I know you have plenty of guests who want your attention. We'll try the food room if that's okay."

"I'll catch up with you in a few minutes. Please make yourselves at home."

He did not hear Tiff's comment as he moved away. "You bet your sweet ass we will."

Susan shook her head. "Maybe we all need a little coffee. If you drink anymore, no tellin' what's gonna happen." She was looking at Tiff and then turned to Margie. "With you, too. Y'all scare me a little bit. I ain't never had to take care of two crazies before."

Tiff was not too drunk to recognize an insult from her sister. "Oh, like you're not as crazy as we are." She looked at Margie. "I'm stuck here with Miss Goodie Two-Shoes and a mass murderer. Let the party begin."

Susan had to laugh at her sister's dramatic description of her situation. Margie did not seem to hear what Tiff said. They ended up standing next to a table covered with a great selection of food. However, they had more tequila on their minds so they made their way to the bar where Dr. James joined them again. The woman who opened the door was mixing the drinks. Dr. James addressed her and made his drink order for the three girls. "My dear, Miss Savannah, these beautiful ladies have come here to add the excitement of youth to our evening. I for one thank them. Please prepare one of your special margaritas for our three special guests."

Susan whispered to Tiff. "That was a little strange."

Tiff did not care. "I think he's cool."

"You would."

"Eat me. Or better still let him eat me." Susan hit Tiff on her arm again.

"I told you to stop hitting me."

"Then stop talkin' so nasty."

The dirty man's name was Dingo, and Officer Boos was tired of all the talk. "You get one hundred dollars right now and the rest when he's sittin' in the backseat of that car." He pointed to his unmarked police car. You have to take us to him right now. No games, no talkin'."

Dingo grinned, showing his disgusting teeth. They looked as dirty as his feet. "No games, no talk. Follow me." Dingo turned away from the two lawmen and walked toward their room. They watched him for a few seconds until he was at the door of the room.

Officer Short did not like what was happening. "Wait a minute you crazy bastard. Stop right there. We said no games. What the hell are you doin'?"

Dingo turned to face them. "He's here in your room. He's been waiting for you."

The lawmen looked at each other and then back at Dingo. Either he was even crazier than they thought or they might be in big trouble. As experienced police officers they both had a bad feeling about their situation. The door of their room opened and a small black man stepped out into the night air. They both drew their guns to defend themselves. Dingo had some advice.

"I'd put those guns down, boys. He just wants to talk, but I can assure you, you will both die of you use those things." When Dingo finished his warning four men stepped from the darkness with four shotguns pointed at the two outmanned officers. Three of the men were black and one was white. The white man was huge with his head shaved clean. The officers slowly placed their guns on the hood of the car. The small black man walked to where they were standing.

"I'm really not sure what to do with you two. The fact that you came back for me as bounty hunters is very disturbing."

Both men were sure they had found Tom Green. David Boos looked at Paul Short. "The waitress called us bounty hunters." He looked back at Tom Green. "Why do you think we're bounty hunters?"

Tom Green moved closer to them. "Come on now, no games, remember?" There was a short moment of silence and then Tom Green continued. "You're not he first ones paid by Butler's daughter to find me. I'm hopin' you are the last."

Tom Green's comment about them being the last was very

unsettling to the two officers. Tom Green had more to say.

"I'm so tired of this. I thought it was over last year, but y'all are the third set of hunters in the last six months. This woman is obsessed with catching and killing me. I guess she loved her daddy and thinks I killed him."

Officer Boos looked at his partner and then back at Tom Green. "You're sayin' you didn't kill Butler."

"It don't matter what I say. Your mind is set and has been for a long time. You will be heroes and make big money if you take me back. My guardian angel set me free and I killed Sheriff Floyd before he could kill me. Runnin' was the only way to stay alive." He stepped even closer to the two defenseless lawmen. "That red-neck cracker poor excuse for a lawman was gonna kill me and my guardian angel appeared once again. After all those years he didn't just forget his friend. As for Shackelford, he just stepped into a buzz saw. That revenge driven woman, Miss Butler, got him killed." He paused with his head down. "I don't owe you two boys all this talk. I ain't sure why I told you this." Tom Green looked away from the two policemen and directed the white man holding a gun on the officers. "Let 'em go. I appreciate your help, but I can't just kill 'em like this."

The huge white man did not like Tom's decision about letting them go. "But, Tom, they gonna try to take ya." He raised his gun and pointed at the two officers again. David Boos' heart jumped. Paul Short had thoughts to reach for his gun and at least have a chance. Tom Green's voice stopped all the aggressive movements

"No, stop. That's it." He looked at the two officers. "I'm sure you're both brave men. If you come to take me I will defend myself and kill you both. But I can't kill another man that has done me no wrong."

The big white man walked to the car and picked up the two guns off the hood. He threw both guns up onto the roof of the nearest building and moved away into the dark. The three black men pointed their guns at the two officers. Tom

Green also moved toward the dark area next to the building. "You'll both die if you come after me again and no one will ever find you. Besides, nothin' can hurt me. I've heard that my guardian angel has returned. He must know your intentions." Tom Green faded into the darkness with the three other men following, one at a time. The last man had to leave them with one more thought.

"Y'all was smart not eatin' that piece of pie."

CHAPTER NINE

It was eight o'clock Sunday morning in every Florida town. The Coffee Cup Restaurant in Ruskin had been open since five thirty for the truckers looking for a good breakfast and some rest before they moved on. The local Catholics would be eating breakfast in two waves. One group came in after the eight-thirty Mass and the second group showed up after the Mass at ten. The Southern Baptist congregation would be there for a late breakfast or early lunch anywhere from twelve to one, depending on how long the preaching went on that particular Sunday morning. The Holiness followers would be the latest group to eat. They would be starving and exhausted from the length of time they had remained in their pews and the verbal and mental thrashing they had taken from a self ordained evangelist.

It was eight o'clock in Vilano Beach. Tiff was the first of the three young women to wake up. It was difficult to open her eyes and focus but she could feel that she was naked and face down in a soft bed. She forced her eyes open and could see she was not alone in the bed. Her sister, Susan, was with her but she was lying there with her head at the end of the bed. Susan was naked, too. Tiff saw the naked body of another woman between her and her sister. She thought it was Margie at first, but a second look told her it was someone else; someone she did not know. Tiff knew she had to wake up her sister, find their clothes, hopefully find Margie and get out of the house. She was afraid because she did not remember anything about the night before. She reached over and shook her sister.

Margie woke up in another room in another bed. Her naked body was covered with a black satin sheet. She was face down, a position she was very familiar with. Her hand was touching the bare back of a man lying next to her. He was asleep with his face turned away from her. It took Margie a few seconds to get her eyes fully opened and to realize where she was. She took her hand off of the man's back and pulled the sheet off her naked body. As she moved to leave the bed the man rolled over toward her and touched her arm.

"Good morning. You okay?"

Margie turned to meet her companion. Her eyes widened to the fullest when she saw the sleepy face of Dr. Roland James smiling at her. She tried to stay as calm as she could and not show her fear and confusion.

"I'm fine. Where's the bathroom?"

He pointed. "Straight ahead."

Margie got out of the bed and walked to the bathroom. She was naked and knew he was watching her as she made her way across the bedroom. Margie was relieved when she closed the bathroom door behind her. She stepped to the mirror to see what she looked like. Margie turned on the sink faucet and splashed cold water into her face. She needed to focus. Margie pulled a big white towel off of the towel rack and wrapped it around her body. She took a deep breath and opened the bathroom door prepared to face her host and new bed partner. When she walked into the bedroom Dr. James was sitting on the edge of the bed wearing a black robe. He smiled.

"Good morning, again."

Margie held the towel in place. She nodded.

"Would you like some breakfast?"

"No, I'm fine." She put her head down. "No, I'm not fine. I can't remember what happened last night. Of course it's obvious what happened but I can't remember any of it. I don't like feeling like this. It ain't right. I know we were together. I can still feel it. It ain't good not to remember."

Dr. James smiled again. "Well, I do like that part about you still feeling it. But I'm sorry you don't remember." He stepped to her but did not touch her. "I can go over what I recall if you'd like a blow by blow description."

Margie took a deep breath. "Do you know where my clothes are?"

He pointed again. "I think most of 'em are on that chair. The silk and lace items seem to be on the floor next to the bed on this side." He pointed a third time. Margie held the towel in place as she gathered her clothes and underwear and walked back toward the bathroom. Dr. James surprised her with a comment as she reached the door.

"I did not put those bruises on your body. They were already there, but I'm sure you knew that."

Margie did not look back at him and closed the bathroom door again. She knew he was right about the bruises.

When Margie came out of the bathroom she was alone in the bedroom. She moved quickly down a hallway and then down the stairs to the first floor. She saw the front door and was going to leave. Dr. James' voice stopped her.

"Please, Margie, don't just leave. Come have some breakfast and then you can go where ever you want. Don't just hurry away."

Margie turned to face him but stayed at the front door. "I don't like the way I feel. Why can't I remember what happened?"

He moved to her side. "I'm not sure. I wish you did. It was a great night as far as I'm concerned. I think you'll feel that way too once you remember. You did have a lot to drink."

She took another deep breath. "I really don't drink very much. Do ya think that's why I can't remember?"

"Sure. It's possible. Especially, if you're not really a big drinker."

Margie hated to admit it but the words came out of her mouth before she could stop them. "Big drinker? I'm not a drinker at all."

He smiled. "Well, you are now. Please, a good breakfast will really make you feel better." He pointed again. "Come join us."

Margie turned and looked into a room where she saw Tiff, Susan and a group of other people sitting at a table eating breakfast. Tiff waved and motioned for her to come into the room. Margie looked back at her host. He smiled.

"It's up to you. If you need to leave, I'll have you taken where ever you want to go. Or you can relax and join us."

Margie was sitting at the table with eight other people. She was glad Tiff and Susan were alright and she was at ease with them there with her. Dr. James sat across from Margie and stared at her the entire time they were eating. The older woman the doctor called, Miss Savannah, was sitting next to Dr. James. She was still wearing her see-through negligee, exposing her huge breasts and the fact she was not wearing any panties. It was interesting attire for a group breakfast. The young woman who was in the bed with Tiff and Susan was young and pretty like the other women. She introduced herself to Margie. Her name was Bella. She was quiet and looked confused and frightened.

There was not much talk during breakfast. Everyone seemed to be recovering from the wild night of alcohol and the possibility of sexual relations. Every guest at the table had a headache. Even Tiff did not have much to say. All three of the other young women were like Margie. They could not remember what happened during the night and early morning. Susan was hoping to talk to Margie and Tiff once they were alone together, but at the moment a free breakfast had her attention.

When the strange breakfast ended Dr. James walked his

four young female houseguests to the front door of his beautiful beach house. Susan and Tiff were the first to say good-bye and thanks for an interesting evening. They walked toward Susan's car, still parked across the street. Bella's car was parked in the driveway. She was the first to hurry directly to her car, back out onto the road and drive away. Susan and Tiff were outside the house ahead of her. Margie did not know how but she was the last one at the door.

Dr. James took her arm before she stepped outside.

"You need to find your way back here sometime today or tonight. We need to talk."

Margie's heart jumped in her chest. She was afraid but tried not to show it. "I don't think so. This whole thing was not good for me. There's something wrong. I can feel it."

He leaned toward her and whispered in her ear. "You told me you need a place to stay. Stay here. You said you need a place to hide. Hide here." Margie trembled as he continued. "You're on the run, girl. Run to me. I'll protect you. You are a rare find and I don't want to be without you. I do hope you remember last night. I, for one, will never forget it."

Margie looked into his dark eyes. She did not like what she saw deep behind. "Thank you for wanting to help me, but I need to go now, they're waiting for me."

He touched her shoulder and could feel her body quiver with fear. "I'll be looking for you before the day's over."

She shook her head. "I'm not comin' back."

He had to whisper one more time. "You killed three members of a band in Jacksonville Beach less than a week ago. I'm sorry you don't remember telling me that last night." Margie stared at her evil host. He handed her a business card. "Go with your friends. If you can't make it back on your own, call me, and I'll come get you. But, be here before dark." He placed his hand on her back and gently pushed her out the door. Margie walked to Susan's car with her legs quivering with fear. Susan was behind the wheel,

Tiff was riding front seat shotgun, so Margie got into the back seat. Susan started the car and drove onto the main road, headed back to St. Augustine. She looked into her inside rearview mirror at Margie.

"What was that all about? I think the ol' Doc has a big crush on our new friend. What do you think, Tiff?"

Tiff smiled. "Well, I know one thing. I woke up in the bed with my sister and a woman I didn't know. I think Miss Margie here, woke up in bed with the man of the house."

Margie had to respond but she knew she had to be careful with her words. "I know how it looks and I know y'all are not going to believe me, but I don't remember one thing about last night. Not, one thing. I've tried, but nothing is there. I don't like it. It scares me. I hate to be such a baby, but I can't help it."

Tiff turned to face Margie in the backseat. "You are far from being a baby. I'm glad you said something." Tiff looked at her sister. "I can't remember anything about last night either. I wasn't gonna say anything about it, because it makes me look like such a drunk. What about you Susan?"

Margie and Tiff were surprised when Susan did not verbally respond to Tiff's question, but she drove the car off of the road and stopped. Susan held on to the steering wheel for a few seconds then turned off the car engine. Tiff was concerned and did not understand.

"What's wrong? You okay? You want me to drive?"

Susan took a deep breath. "No, I'm fine. The last thing I remember from last night is hearing him tell the big tittied bartender to fix us those special margaritas. I thought it was just me, but now I think the ol' Doc uses drugs on selected guests. I think him and titty woman have a shitty little game goin' on here. He finds young women, she helps him drug 'em and they both take advantage. And how stupid are we? Just how easy was it to get us there? No telling what they did to us and who did it. I don't think we'll ever remember so we'll never know. I do know one thing they did to me because my ass is on fire. It's our own damn fault, but I do hate that sack of shit doctor.

Margie couldn't believe it when Tiff burst out laughing. Susan was mad at Tiff's reaction. "Oh, you think that's funny, do ya?"

Tiff forced herself to stop laughing. "I'm not laughin' at you sayin' your ass is burnin'. I'm laughin' at the fact mine's on fire, too." Tiff looked back at Margie. "How 'bout you Margie, butt burnin'?"

Susan burst into laughter with Tiff. "Stop makin' me laugh, damn it. It hurts worse when I laugh. My stomach muscles are sore. My butt hurts. I've got a tequila headache and you are makin' me laugh. Stop it."

Tiff wanted Margie to answer her question. "Well, are you in pain or not?"

Margie nodded. "Yes, it's awful. I was bleeding earlier when I was in the bathroom." The car was silent for a few seconds. Margie broke the quiet moment. "You two need to know that I'm in big trouble. You probably don't need to be with me. I should be on my way out of town, but I can't let this man get away with what he did to me. He threatened me at the door that if I didn't come back later today he would call the police. I must have told him things last night." The sisters were wide eyed and listening. "I'm goin' back there tonight and make sure he pays for our three burnin' asses."

Tiff held back another outburst of laughter at Margie's burning butt comment, but did share her thought. "You did kill somebody, didn't ya? You wasn't makin' that up, was ya?"

Margie put her head down. Tiff looked at her sister as Susan started the car and drove out onto the road. Susan had to get her thoughts together. "Come home with us Margie and we'll sort this thing out together."

It was nine o'clock when Officers David Boos and Paul Short drove up to the Coffee Cup Restaurant. They had not decided their course of action concerning the fugitive, Tom Green. The threat and warning they received the night before was heavy on their minds. Paul Short was curious about returning to the not so friendly Pie House. He waited for David Boos to turn off the car engine.

"Tell me again why we came back to this place where we are not wanted at all. I don't think I can eat here, can you?"

"I'm not sure why myself. I just think this is the place for us to be today. Besides, I'd like to talk to that waitress about Tom Green knowing where we were."

A young teenage hostess escorted the two policemen to a small corner table. They sat down as she dropped breakfast menus on the table. "You gents want to start with coffee?"

David Boos nodded his head. "Yes, please."

Paul Short shook his head. "Nothin' for me, thank you."

David Boos smiled. "You think that little girl's gonna poison us?"

"We've both seen how crazy it is around here. Are you so sure she won't?"

Margie told her story of sexual abuse and defending herself. She felt it had happened again to her at the hands of the handsome Dr. James. And now, he was threatening her survival.

Susan and Tiff had listened and nodded in agreement that the doctor had abused her and they were victims, too. However, they were not going to return to the beach house for the revenge that Margie was considering. Susan expressed her thought once Margie expressed her intent.

"You don't need to go back there at all. If you go back there, you will be caught you know it. Or he could hurt you even more and turn you in anyway."

Margie knew Susan was right, but she wanted her revenge. It had become part of her personality. Susan was sorry their new friend had told them her story. It was information she and Tiff did not need to know. Susan knew they needed to distance themselves from this woman on the run. Margie felt the fear coming from Susan.

"I'm sorry that I put you two in this situation. I didn't

mean for this to happen. Trouble seems to follow me and I make terrible decisions. I need to go, now. Thank you both for your kindness." Susan and Tiff would not betray Margie, but they were glad she was gone and they could go back to their mistake filled lives. They could only blame themselves for being in the abusive situation.

Margie was not surprised when the two sisters said "good-bye". She could see the relief in their eyes. Margie left them, walked a few blocks and stopped in front of a small general store. It reminded her of her store in Mayport. Margie had to smile as she walked toward the small building.

She stopped at a pay phone next to the store, took out the business card Dr. James had given her, picked up the phone and dialed the number on the card. A woman answered.

"Dr. James' residence."

"This is Margie. Tell Dr. James that I need a ride."

Susan and Tiff would stay out of the bars and night life for a few days. They would be back in action as the week end came near but for now the two wild sisters would lay-low and try to stay out of trouble.

Margie's heart raced and she was afraid when a white Mercedes Benz rolled up next to her. It had dark tinted windows. Her heart raced even faster when the car stopped and the driver's side window went down. Dr. James' female companion, Miss Savannah, was driving the white chariot of possible doom.

"Hello Margie, get in. Sit up front with me."

Margie nodded and walked to the other side of the car.

They were both silent during the ride back to the beach house. Margie tried not to look at the woman, but she did cut her eyes in the woman's direction once or twice during the ride. The woman was half naked with a see-through blouse, revealing that she wore no bra to cover her huge breasts. She wore a bikini bottom tied on each hip and no shoes. The woman broke the silence when she saw Margie looking her way.

"Pardon my dress, Margie. I was sunning by the pool when he asked me to pick you up."

Margie looked out the front window as they pulled into the driveway of the beach house.

In a matter of minutes Margie was sitting in Dr. James' big living room with the evil physician and his big breasted companion. Margie was nervous but for some reason she knew the feeling would pass once she put her plan of revenge into motion. Dr. James was controlling the conversation.

"You made the right decision, Margie. I knew you would." He touched her hand. "We're going to be great business partners."

Margie hated the smirk of a smile on the woman's face and the arrogance Dr. James had when he spoke to her. She knew they were the only ones in the house. It was the perfect opportunity for her to surprise them. Dr. James had more to say.

"We're going to start right away, Margie. I have two good friends coming over later and they are excited about meeting you. I'm sure you will blow their socks off." He smiled. "And I do mean that literally."

Margie did not really hear his little nasty play on words. She was thinking that she should kill him first because "titty woman" would be the weaker and easier victim. The shock of her attack on the doctor would give Margie the time to make her second attack. Margie knew it had to be done while they were all together.

Dr. James had more to tell Margie as he turned to his companion. "Now, tomorrow night, Margie, you will have the pleasure of allowing a group of my good friends to watch you and Miss Savannah enjoy each other's physical attributes and talents. Isn't her body superb?" He touched Miss Savannah on the shoulder. Margie looked into her eyes as Dr. James continued. "I have a feeling you two are going to be our biggest attraction. You're going to love the way Miss Savannah works."

Dr. James directed his next words to Margie's new sex partner. "Go ahead and make the call. I don't think Margie will need any instructions. She's pretty much a natural at this stuff. After the call, take Margie upstairs and get her cleaned up and dressed properly."

Margie was only a few feet from her abuser. The time was right. She was no longer nervous. Margie was made for revenge. Dr. James smiled as Margie stood up. He did not see the flash of the blade as Margie chopped at his throat with her white pearl handle, split blade knife. The blade was made to cut deep and wide. Dr. James felt a burning sensation as his hot blood poured down his neck and onto his chest.

Miss Savannah did not have time to react or leave her seat as Margie turned and took another swing with the deadly weapon. The sharp blade hit the woman across her face between her bottom lip and her chin. She screamed and grabbed the injured area with one hand. Margie sliced again cutting her forearm and then slashing down her breasts. The deep cut suffered by Dr. James was fatal and he had already collapsed, falling forward and crashing head first into a glass top coffee table. Margie knew he was dead. None of the wounds on the woman were death blows so Margie had to continue her vicious attack until her revenge was complete.

It would only be one day before the housekeeper found the two dead bodies. Susan and Tiff would read the headlines in the paper about the brutal death of the prominent doctor and his companion. They knew their new friend, Margie, had avenged them all.

CHAPTER TEN

When the Greyhound bus made its first stop on the outskirts of Fernandina Beach, Margie looked out of the dirty bus window and saw a sign: Welcome to American Beach.

She also saw another sign next to a big three story house that read: Rooms for Rent. Margie did not know why, but she picked up her bag of belongings and got off the bus in American Beach.

In only a minute or so Margie stood on the front porch of the big three story house and knocked on the wooden facing of the screen door. She could feel the vibration of someone walking in the house toward the front door. An overweight white woman opened the door and peered out the screen. She had a beautiful round face and it was obvious the woman was very attractive in the days before the pounds were added to her frame. She smiled with white and straight teeth. Her low cut flowered blouse exposed and introduced her huge breasts with a ten inch cleavage line as a hint of what was underneath. Margie's eyes left the woman's smile and followed the cleavage line.

"Now, ain't you a pretty thing. Yes ma'am, may I help you?"

Margie smiled. "I'm interested in renting a room for a few days."

The woman opened the screen door. "I do have one room that will be ready in a little while. I was just changin' the bed sheets when you knocked. Come on in." The lady opened the screen door wider as Margie walked into the house. "I'm Miss Amelia, mama named me after this island."

"I'm Margie, mama named me after her sister."

Miss Amelia walked slowly up the stairs with Margie following behind. Miss Amelia did not talk. It was a hard climb for the big woman. Margie's room was on the second floor of the huge house. The second floor hallway was lined on both sides with single bedrooms, four on each side of the long hall. Margie saw other rooms on the first floor before they climbed the stairs. She was amazed at the fact there were even more rooms on the third floor. She figured there were at least twenty-five bedrooms in this huge boarding house.

Just before Margie followed Miss Amelia into her room, she looked into the bedroom directly across the hall. The door was opened slightly and Margie saw movement. She saw the back of a young man. He was facing away from her. He wore faded blue dungarees with no shirt. He had a full head of dark curly hair. The young man must have felt Margie's stare as he turned to face her. He nodded, smiled and covered his manly chest as he pulled a black t-shirt over his upper body. Miss Amelia's voice took Margie away from her vision.

"The first day is six dollars. After that it's five dollars a day. If you pay in advance for five or more days its four dollars a day. It's more of a bargain if you stay longer."

Margie reached into her pocket and took out a thin fold of bills. She counted out six one dollar bills and handed them to Miss Amelia.

"Thank you, but I'll probably just stay tonight."

Miss Amelia nodded and took the money. "That's fine Margie, thank you and welcome to the island."

Margie looked back to see the young man again. His bedroom door was closed.

Miss Amelia left the room and before she closed the door Margie saw a young girl join Miss Amelia in the hallway. The girl was young but strikingly beautiful. Exotic would be the term when describing her. The girl looked at Margie but did not smile as Miss Amelia closed the door. Margie would fall asleep for few hours but wake up to laughter and noises in the hall.

Margie got dressed and went downstairs. Miss Amelia was talking to two distinguished looking older men in the living room area. Miss Amelia nodded but did not speak. Margie stepped out onto the small front porch. An early evening breeze touched her face. It felt good as if it was telling Margie to relax, better days were coming her way. Her moment on the porch ended as Miss Amelia and the two men walked out the front door and joined her. She turned to face them. Miss Amelia walked the two men into the front yard and they got into a big black car and drove away. She did not introduce her new guest to the two visitors.

"You hungry, girl?"

Margie was surprised by the question. "Yes ma'am, I am."

"Best Bar-B-Q anywhere is right down that road 'bout a hundred yards up in the woods. It's worth the walk. I promise. Just tell Ollie I sent you there and he'll take good care of ya. He's kinda been my man forever. He's the only man that has ever really satisfied me, if ya know what I mean. And the bastard can cook, too. You find a man that can fuck and cook, you really got somethin'."

Margie smiled. She had never heard a woman talk that way. "I'll try it. I do like some good Bar-B-Q."

"Don't we all, girl? Don't we all?"

Margie enjoyed her pulled pork sandwich with fried onion rings and crispy French fries. The iced-tea was as sweet as she had ever tasted. Ollie was kind when she introduced herself but stayed in the kitchen while she was there. He was a big man, not fat, just big. Margie found herself wondering what Ollie had in his pants that was able to satisfy a woman like Miss Amelia. She shook those thoughts from her head and ate her Bar-B-Q.

Thirty minutes later, Margie had no idea why she was sitting on a bar stool in the Honey Dripper Lounge on American Beach near Fernandina, Florida. As she looked around the room, it only took her a few seconds to realize she was the only white person in the building. Miss Amelia had suggested Margie go there for an evening of good food, good drinks and great music and a full dance floor. Miss Amelia left out the fact that the Honey Dripper was a black honky tonk. Margie was nervous and her heart jumped when a huge black man stepped up from behind the bar.

"You sure ya in the right place ma'am?"

Margie could feel her heart pounding. She wanted to show she knew what she was doing and where she was. "Of course, I'm in the right place. This is the Honey Dripper, isn't it?"

The huge bartender smiled with big snow white perfect teeth. "Ya just seemed to be a little lost ma'am, but I guess I was wrong. What ya drinkin'?"

Margie wanted him to know she belonged there. "I'd like a margarita, on the rocks with salt on the rim."

The bartender smiled and nodded his head. "Well ma'am, I ain't made one in a long time, but I think I can do it."

Margie nodded, too. "Thank you. That would be nice."

Margie looked around the room for a few seconds before the bartender returned with her drink. He placed it on the bar in front of her.

"Here ya go, ma'am. If it ain't a good one let me know. I don't want no unhappy customers."

He stood there waiting for her to take a sip. He smiled. "I need to know, ma'am."

Margie picked up the glass and took a sip and touched her tongue on the layer of salt on the rim. She held the glass away from her mouth. "It's perfect. Thank you."

The bartender's eyes lit up and his smile was the biggest and brightest so far.

"Thank you, ma'am. That's gonna be my special drink tonight. I always have a special that everyone tries. It's margarita night at the Honey Dripper." He smiled again. "And you ma'am drink free all night."

Margie's heart was still racing but not so much from fear but from the tequila, salt and excitement coming from the huge black man. He turned to help another customer. She could only think of one thing to say.

"You have the most beautiful teeth I've ever seen."

He turned back to her. "Thank ya ma'am. My mama used to say that to me. You just gave me a great memory." He seemed to be thinking about something for a second or so. "I'm Bunker. They call me Bunker."

"I'm Margie. Pleased to meet you, Mr. Bunker."

"Same here." Bunker smiled at her manners and moved to the other customers. As he approached the couple sitting at the bar the woman smiled and lifted her arms out to Bunker. "Oh Bunker, you have the prettiest teeth I've ever seen."

The few customers in the room all laughed at the mocking moment. Bunker shook his head and tried not to smile. Margie's heart raced and she tried not to look at the other customers as a beautiful black woman sat down next to Margie.

"He ain't never been called Mr. Bunker. I know he liked you sayin' that. And talkin' 'bout his pretty teeth, you just somethin', ain't ya?"

Margie wasn't sure how to respond to the woman's words. She smiled as the woman surprised her with her next question. "And what the hell is a pretty white woman like you doin' in this black establishment?"

While Margie was afraid to answer, Bunker stepped up to the bar where they were sitting.

"Now, Ruby. This here's Margie. She's sittin' here minding her own business and drinking the Honey Dripper drink special of the evening. I think you could have a nice conversation with her if you gave it a try."

Ruby shook her head as she answered Bunker but looked at Margie. "No Bunker, she's too pretty and way too white to be in here with all the crazy niggas gonna show up here tonight."

Ruby's stare was unsettling to Margie but she had to be sure to act like she was not bothered by her aggressive words or intimidating eyes. The woman seemed familiar to Margie at first but she would not comment on her thoughts. Margie just wanted to stay in shouting distance of her new friend, Bunker.

Ruby had more to add to the uncomfortable feeling raging in Margie's body and head. "I ain't even had a drink yet and I can see this one is got big trouble written all over that beautiful face. She brings pain with her." Ruby leaned in closer to Margie and whispered. "We go a lot in common, don't we white girl. We might be sisters in a way."

Margie wanted to have her say, but could not find the courage to defend her self. Her body trembled on the inside. She was relieved as Ruby moved away from the bar and went to sit at a table. Two men quickly joined Ruby at the table and seemed to take her attention away from Margie. Margie looked at Bunker.

"I don't think she likes me. Please tell me she won't shoot me later on tonight."

Bunker smiled. "Well if anybody would, it would probably be Ruby."

Margie took another sip of her drink. "Are you serious? That's not funny."

"I won't let her shoot you, I promise. Ruby's a regular here. She lives in a place they call Cosmo over near Fort Caroline. It's the only black neighborhood in that area. They say she's a man killer." Margie's eyes lit up and she took another drink while Bunker talked about Ruby. "She ain't never talked about it with me but folks say she's had a crazy life. They say she used to dance for white men and sell her body. You should see her dance. Men can't stay away from her. It's like magic. Like she puts 'em under a spell of some kind. Folks around here who come from the islands say she knows the Craft when it comes to seduction."

Margie had to interrupt. "Has she ever put you under her spell, Mr. Bunker?"

He had too smile again as he moved to a new customer. "Every time she dances."

Miss Amelia was walking down the long hallway on the third floor of her boarding house. She looked into each room as she made her way down the carpeted hall. There were seven small bedrooms on both sides. As Miss Amelia passed each room a young painted woman wearing all colors of night wear stepped to each one of the fourteen doors. When Miss Amelia reached the end of the long hallway she stopped, turned back to face the young beautiful faces. She had a huge smile on her pretty fat face.

"You girls look wonderful. It's Saturday night. The mill workers got paid. Suzette just sent word that the Palace Saloon is full of Mayport sailors and they have a bus to shuttle them around. She's makin' a deal right now to have that bus head this way when they get drunk enough. It will be a great night once the gray Navy bus is sittin' in front of our porch."

The fourteen young women were all smiles and goose bumps. It was obvious they liked what they were doing. Miss Amelia added to their excitement.

"Let's make some big money tonight, girls. Let's make 'em so happy they can't stay away." The young ladies actually cheered all at once as if Miss Amelia was giving the team a pep talk before the big game.

The Honey Dripper Lounge was filling up with locals who were the regular customers. Bunker was busy and Margie did not bother him as she sipped her free drink. She did not look at Ruby for fear the witch of seduction would be looking back at her. Bunker stepped close to her as he opened a bottle of Schlitz Beer for a customer. He had more information about Ruby.

"They also say Ruby was a mate to the devil, or a man who thought he was the devil."

Margie said it again. "Are you serious?"

"Folks think he held her captive because of her love making abilities. I'm tellin' ya, the stories that follow Ruby are full of the unnatural. They say the man got killed in Mayport one night by some woman over there folks seem to fear. He was gonna steal a baby and use the child for devil stuff."

Margie's heart went crazy in her chest. She knew who Ruby was, now. She had to turn to look at the black woman to be sure it was her. Margie's heart started beating so hard she could feel it against her blouse when she realized Ruby was looking directly at her, too. Margie recognized Ruby but Ruby was yet to recognize Margie. Their stare was broken when the juke box went silent and the house lights in the lounge went down. The crowd began to clap, whistle and cheer.

Margie looked around and could hear the sound of an instrument playing behind the noise of the crowd. The sounds of praise faded as they all listened to the sound of a blues saxophone. A single spotlight flashed on a small round stage as a young white man's cheeks puffed and blew air into a black mouth piece making the sweetest yet haunting sounds.

Bunker leaned toward Margie. "I should have realized you was here to see 'The Man'."

Margie did not understand. She turned to the light and the music. Her eyes widened and her heart raced even harder when she saw the young man she had seen earlier in the bedroom across from hers at the boarding house.

His given name was David Lott, but the players of the night called him "Moonlight Charlie". He was a true contradiction to his original status and place in the world. David was born to Bernard and Mary Veronica Lott. His father was a wealthy Jacksonville banker with a mansion on the St. Johns River. His mother was a beautiful true upper class socialite who painted watercolors of the river and played the piano and cello.

While daddy made money and mama made new rich friends, David was raised by a black nanny he called Miss Juliana. She was like a second mother to David and she actually spent more time with him than Mary Veronica did. During his relationship with Miss Juliana, David was introduced to the great musicians of the time.

On Sunday she would take David to her church where he would hear gospel songs that taught him more and more about music and life. Miss Juliana's cousin, Cato, worked as the grounds keeper for the Lott family and he taught David to play the guitar and saxophone. David took to the two instruments as if they had always been a part of him. He was a natural, playing the music by ear. It was obvious David Lott was born to play. Cato would have David listen to Charlie Parker play the saxophone and David would mimic the sound to the letter.

As David matured, he left his life in the mansion on the river and wanted to share his music and talents with the world. He traveled through Georgia and Florida playing in honky tonks and on stages at the state fairs. Because of his background and relationship with Miss Juliana and Cato, David took his sound to more black establishments. After a year on the road, he returned to play at the Honey Dripper, his favorite honky tonk. It was where they first named him Moonlight Charlie. It had something to do with how his music moved his listeners when the moon was full. He was good anytime he played but he was great on a full moon. They said the full moon moved him like it moved the tides.

David liked having a suitable name. His parents did not approve of his late night honky tonk appearances so being Moonlight Charlie saved the Lott family name from the embarrassment of raising a true honky tonk man.

He had a bond with nature and skinny dipped in the Atlantic Ocean after he played for the soulful crowds that filled the honky tonks near the Georgia and Florida coastlines. He was never alone on his naked swims. There was always a willing young southern girl who would take off her clothes and get wet with Moonlight Charlie. He considered the activity as a ritual, both sexual and spiritual.

Most women, young and old, were attracted to David. His looks, southern charm, and ability to move folks with his music were his calling cards and many women answered the call. He was confident and had learned a great deal from his many sexual encounters. His specialty was his skinny dipping rituals.

Moonlight Charlie had been given his first taste of marijuana a few years earlier when he was playing one night at the Blue Moon Tavern in Mayport, Florida. After he played that night, a young black woman had taken a fancy to him and on their way to the Seminole Beach swimming hole for a naked moonlight swim, she had him stop at Aunt Matilda's place, where Zulmary sold David his first bag of marijuana. It would not be his last. That night at the Mayport swimming hole with the young black woman and Zulmary's home grown weed, was one of David's better nights. When he was in the area he often returned to Miss Matilda's before her death and the burning of her business. He had even had a sexual moment with Zulmary one night but he could not remember much about it. Zulmary had that effect on the men she touched.

With his artistic talents, handsome features and charming personality, Moonlight Charlie was a true lover, but not a fighter. With the women wanting him, the men hating him, being a fighter would have come in handy now and then.

There was an incident when Moonlight Charlie was appearing at Strickland's outside deck bar on First Street in Jacksonville Beach, Florida. A beautiful young woman had been watching him most of the night. It was obvious to David she was moved by this music and charm. He had seen that reaction many times. She was with a huge young sailor when she first arrived, but he left and she stayed at the bar. David was dying for a taste of Zulmary's exotic plant so when he took his break he walked down to the beach to satisfy his need. Strickland's was located fifty yards from the shore of the Atlantic Ocean. As soon as David fired up his mellow stick, the young woman from the bar stepped out of the darkness.

"How 'bout a drag?" David handed her the joint and watched her suck in the dulling smoke. She handed it back to him. "Thanks. I'm Silvia. You know you've been drivin' me crazy all night, don't ya?"

Moonlight Charlie knew how to answer such a question. "And you know you've been drivin' me crazy, too."

Silvia smiled. "How long before you have to go back?"

Moonlight Charlie took another drag. "Pretty soon. I got one more set and I'll be done. Maybe, we can take a swim later. I've got a room for the night at Miss Dunn's if you're interested."

Silvia did not need very much encouragement. She had a much better idea. "If it works out, that would be nice. But I can't keep my hands off you and I can't wait. I don't want to let a moment get away in case there ain't no other chance."

Silvia grabbed Moonlight Charlie and kissed him with fire on her lips and tongue. He hardly had any time to return her passion when Silvia dropped to her knees in the white beach sand, unbuckled his belt, unzipped his pants and pulled his manhood out into the night air. He was deep into her mouth before he could catch his breath. The suction was like no other he had ever felt. Moonlight Charlie allowed his new friend to take all he had to give. While she was working, he put his hand down her blouse and squeezed one of her breasts and then the other. Silvia moaned when he pinched and pulled her nipples. She did not stop sucking until his tank was empty.

Silvia stood up and wiped the edges of her mouth. "Maybe we'll take that swim later. If not, I'm pretty happy with our first time together."

Moonlight Charlie thought, *If you're happy, I'm happy,*

but did not say it out loud. Before he could respond, Silvia was walking away. She turned back to him. "What room are you in?"

David was light headed but managed to answer her. "Seven. It's on the beach side." Silvia was not at the bar when he returned.

Moonlight Charlie finished his final set and decided Silvia had been enough woman for the night. His mellow state of mind added to his need to go to his room and get some sleep. Miss Dunn's was only a few blocks away.

Moonlight Charlie had a way of finding and staying in the interesting boarding houses where ever he was. They were always low rent, had a bad reputation and were havens for the ladies of the evening. If he did not bring a woman back to his room, there was always one close by if he was so inclined.

He placed is guitar case and saxophone case on the concrete and stuck the key into the lock on the door to room number seven. As he turned the key, something hit him on the back of the head. David went down to his knees and fell forward into the door. Someone picked him up and turned him around. He could see the white uniform of a sailor. David took a blow to his right eye and went down again as his attacker talked to him through clenched teeth. As he talked, the sailor kicked David after every complete sentence. Each kick gave emphasis to his message.

"You think you can come in here, play a little music, drug and force your way on our women. You pretty boys think there ain't no consequences for ya. You just do whatever you want and move on. Well, that ain't so tonight, sport." David took his fourth kick to his ribs and stomach. "The sailor had more to say but he stopped kicking his victim." You know I could just kill ya right here and nobody would care or know anything about it?"

David could not talk, but he knew the sailor was right. The thought of dying right there added to his fear and pain. He waited for the final blow to come from his assailant, but he watched the sailor's shiny, black patent leather shoes move away.

David did not move for a few minutes. He was afraid the sailor was waiting to attack him again if he tried to get up. When he did sit up he leaned against the door and took a deep breath causing immediate pain to his bruised and battered rib cage. He looked up and saw the key still hanging in the lock to the door. He knew he needed to get into the room for his own safety and well-being. It was a struggle, but he got to his feet, picked up both cases, unlocked the door and slowly moved into the room. As he put the cases on the floor he pushed the door, trying to close it. The door was pulled open again and someone entered the dark room with him. They closed and locked the door.

David's heart screamed with fear as he prepared to be beaten to death by the violent and angry sailor. A soft voice filled the dark room.

"Oh Moonlight! I'm so sorry about Ned. He gets so crazy jealous. I didn't think he would come find you. I had to lie to him about you forcin' me and the weed. I was scared he was gonna beat the hell out of me, too. I didn't think he'd come hurt you like this."

David tried to absorb all her ranting words but he was in such pain and shock that he only heard half of what she said. He was able to force out a few words.

"You told him where I was stayin'?"

Her eyes lit up. "I had to. He was Indian burnin' my arm. That shit hurts. It was the only way to make him stop. Look how red my arm still is." She held her arm up in the dark. "If you ever had one, you'd understand I had to tell."

David moved to the bed and sat down. Silvia moved with him. She reached over to the night stand next to the bed and turned on the lamp. David squinted his eyes at the bright light. Silvia made a face when she saw the damage to David's eye. It was not cut, but it was swollen and turning black already. She touched his face.

"I'm so sorry. Please forgive me. It all just got too crazy for me. I wanted to make him stop when he was kicking you, but I didn't want him to see me."

David could not believe his ears. "You watched him beatin' me out there?"

"Once I realized he might come find you I thought I could get here first to warn you, but I was too late so I just hid in the dark."

They were both silent for a few seconds. David lay back onto the bed and took another painful deep breath. Silvia stood next to the bed looking down at him. David managed a few more words.

"I think you need to get away from here. If he finds you here, he'll kill us both sure enough."

Silvia shook her head. "I need to stay here and take care of you. It's my fault. Besides, Ned don't own me."

David begged to differ. "You might think not, but I'm pretty sure he thinks he does."

Silvia smiled and began to undress. David had not seen her naked during her brief but outstanding oral attack on the beach. He was afraid that at any second the door was going to be torn off the hinges and big, crazy Ned was going to join them. As Silvia stripped, David had to watch. She showed her big round, firm breasts first. He loved them. Then he saw her flat stomach. She turned to tease him as she pulled her pants down, exposing her rock hard butt and legs. Silvia was a physical treasure and Moonlight Charlie would not pass up such a find.

During that night together, Silvia's sexual activity and talents actually took away his fear and pain. He was so busy waiting for her next performance that he understood why a man might kill for her. She did everything and even things Moonlight Charlie had never experienced. She was non-stop and almost relentless in her effort to please. When David had nothing left and was soft, she would still suck on him and work her own body until he was up and ready again. While she waited for him, she pleasured herself and made sure he was watching her every move. David knew she was a dangerous woman but at the moment he did not care.

Sometime during the painful and wonderful night, they both fell asleep. When David woke up, Silvia was gone. He was in great pain from the sex they had and the beating he took, but he forced himself to get up, get dressed and get out. Moonlight Charlie knew he would see Silva again. At least he hoped he would.

The gray Navy bus was parked in the front driveway of Miss Amelia's boarding house. It was empty. Even the bus driver was in the house having sexual relations with one of the young women in a third floor bedroom. All fourteen bedrooms had some manner of sexual activity in progress. The living room down stairs had ten other young sailors impatiently waiting their turn for that walk up the stairs to the third floor. They could hardly wait to make the heavenly stairway climb to the angels willing to share their sexual favors with a paying customer. Miss Amelia was moving among the ten young men trying to assure them they would soon be in the arms of a beautiful woman with their utmost desires being filled and fed.

Miss Amelia kept them busy with sweet tea and decorative cookies. That was much cheaper than serving alcoholic beverages and pastries. The idea was making money, not spending it. She also gave the group of sexually hungry men an up close and personal look at her incredible breast cleavage with her big dark nipples pressing against her silky blouse. The sight of her outstanding assets only fueled the fire in their loins.

Miss Amelia would stand close to one of the young men and be sure she touched him, or brushed her breasts against him. Sometimes she would allow the young men to touch her breasts with a quick squeeze as she moved away. One of the young men tried to lick Miss Amelia's cleavage line as she stood close to him. She smiled and moved away.

"Miss Amelia would ruin you for any other woman, son.

I don't want that on my conscience. You better stick with the pretty little girls upstairs. You could get hurt bad between these legs."

The group of nine other young men exploded into laughter as Miss Amelia turned to meet two of the sailors coming down from their adventure on the third floor.

She moved to the bottom step as they approached her. "You boys didn't stay too long up there. The more money, the longer you stay."

The two young men moved to the waiting area and talked to some of the other men awaiting their turn. One of the men was disgusted and pleased at the same time.

"She was beautiful and was doin' everything I wanted. Hell, I ain't even had to tell her nothing. She just knew what I wanted. I only had money for fifteen minutes. I thought I had two tens left in my pocket, but I musta spent one at the bar. I need to borrow some more money."

The other sailors liked what he was saying about the way he was treated, but the thought of limiting their cash was out of the question and not considered by any of them.

Miss Amelia escorted two new paying customers up the steps to the third floor to replace the two who had run out of time and money. As the trio moved up the stairs one of the men in the living room had questions for the two veterans.

"How much she charge ya, Sammy?"

It was easy to see Sammy was still excited. "It's ten dollars for fifteen minutes and they got little timers on the table next to the bed. I think they got them egg timers. I only had ten dollar dammit."

"They tell ya when ya first go in. They want you to know when the timer rings, that's it." Sammy was really in a sweat. "Let's see. Ten dollars for every fifteen minutes. But you can get a bargain and pay thirty five dollars for an hour. When I come back, I'm gettin' that hour."

The eight young men still waiting all checked their pockets to see how much time they could individually afford to pay. Sammy's firsthand experience and financial deficit was golden information for all the first timers.

Miss Amelia appeared at the door showing more of her breasts. Another paying customer had returned with her. He joined the others. Miss Amelia smiled. "Who's next? I don't remember how you boys were lined up to go. Be honest, now boys. Ya mama wouldn't want ya tellin' lies to Miss Amelia. Who's next?"

One of the bigger and obviously older young men stepped up. None of the others protested his move toward Miss Amelia. She took his muscular arm, but he did not move with her. She stopped and looked into his deep black eyes. Miss Amelia was surprised when her heart jumped and the young man spoke to her.

"I can have a girl anytime. How much to be with the madam of the house for half an hour?"

Miss Amelia was not sure what to make of the young man's financial challenge. She was there to make money. This was an unusual chance to do so or scare the young man away. She tried to hide her nervous quivers.

"I'm flattered at your offer."

He smiled. "You can be flattered if you want, but I'm pretty sure you've taught those girls upstairs everything they know about how to please us. I want to spend time with the teacher, not the student."

Miss Amelia knew how to end his pursuit. "It'll cost you one hundred dollars every fifteen minutes with no specials for an hour."

The young man smiled his biggest smile so far. "I'll take that half hour."

Miss Amelia's heart raced behind her huge beautiful breasts as the young man pulled two one-hundred dollar bills from his pants pocket and handed the money to her.

The room was quiet. She took the money then offered her hand to the young man. This time he moved with her to the bottom of the stairs. Miss Amelia yelled down the hallway.

"Ellie, come up front."

In a few seconds a young beautiful woman met them at the stairs. Ellie would be eighteen soon and was no doubt the most beautiful female in the house. Miss Amelia was Ellie's only family. Her father was a white sailor just passing through the area nineteen years ago and her mother was one of Miss Amelia's first workers. Her name was Jade and she was half black and half Chinese. It was a beautiful combination for making babies. Ellie was the result of the brief encounter and union. Jade had died of complications soon after Ellie was born.

The sailors in waiting all took deep breaths when they saw her. The young man still holding Miss Amelia's arm could not believe how perfect Ellie was. Miss Amelia had chores for the young beauty.

"Ellie, go upstairs and get Marli to come down and keep things movin' down here. Tell her I'll be back in a half hour." She smiled and patted the young man's hand that was still on her arm. Then she addressed Ellie again. "Then, go over to the bar and tell Bunker to come as early as he can."

The young girl nodded her perfect head and ran up the stairs. Miss Amelia turned to her handsome customer.

"My room's right down the hall." She led the way and he followed.

Margie was drinking her second free margarita and found herself a little light headed and absolutely mesmerized by Moonlight Charlie and his music. It was different. It was moving and sincere. It was more than music. It had substance. It had taken her away from her thoughts of Ruby. Bunker stepped up to her. He knew Margie was taken by the music and the maker. Bunker's voice startled Margie.

"He's the perfect example of that ol' black sayin'."

Margie's heart was still racing. She turned and focused on Bunker. "What old saying is that?"

Bunker smiled with his beautiful white teeth and hesitated for a few seconds before he gave her the answer and shared a philosophical moment with his new white lady friend.

"You can't teach 'cool'. You're either born with it or ya ain't. That white boy was born 'cool'. Everybody knows he's got some black in 'im from somewhere."

Margie turned away from Bunker and looked at Moonlight Charlie as he sat on a stool playing his guitar and singing to the grateful crowd.

Moonlight Charlie took his first break and sat down at the bar a few stools away from Margie. When he sat down he nodded to her and said. "Don't I know you?"

Bunker stepped up to the bar. "Now, I know that the one and only Moonlight Charlie must have a better line than that one. That one's ol' as grits. I was just tellin' this lady how cool you were and you come up here with that bull-shit. You makin' me look bad, son."

Moonlight Charlie had to smile at Bunker's ranting. "No man, I mean it. I've seen her before. I really have."

Margie smiled and nodded at Bunker. "It's true. We did not meet, but we saw each other over at the boarding house. Our rooms are across the hall from each other."

Charlie's face lit up. "That's it. I did see you. I'm Moonlight Charlie." He smiled again. "Actually, I'm David, but everybody calls me Moonlight Charlie. Whatever you want to call me is fine with me."

Margie was still light headed and tried to smile. "I'm just Margie, nothing extra. Do I call you Charlie, or Moonlight, or both? What do you want me to call you? I need to settle on one."

"I think I'd like you to call me David. Nice to meet you, Margie. Welcome to American Beach and the Honey Dripper Lounge."

The young mixed blood beauty, Ellie, walked into the Honey Dripper and went directly to the bar. All the local customers knew who the young girl was and where she was from. They all marveled at her beauty. The men wanted her and the women wanted to look like her. The men all knew that Bunker was on Miss Amelia's payroll as a protector of the house, the girls and Ellie. No man, knowing about Bunker, would purposely invite his wrath. The young girl stepped to the bar. Margie noticed David was the first one to acknowledge the young girl.

"Hey, Ellie."

Ellie flashed a beautiful smile at Moonlight Charlie. "Hey." She looked behind the bar as Bunker approached her.

"What's up, pretty girl?"

"Miss Amelia said for me to tell you to come any time when you can. They're pretty busy and she needs ya."

"I'll go back with ya. My back-up just came in." He stepped to Margie. "One more drink, ma'am, before I go?"

"No, I'm fine. Thank you, Bunker. You have been so kind to me."

"No problem." Bunker turned to the replacement bartender. "This lady drinks free, ya hear me?"

The new tender looked at Margie. "You got it, Bunker."

As Bunker walked away with Ellie, Margie heard Ellie say to Bunker, "Miss Amelia's a working girl tonight."

Margie turned to David. "Where's Bunker going and who was that beautiful girl?"

David had the answer. "They're going over to Miss Amelia's. Ellie lives there. Miss Amelia's the only family the girl has. Her mother worked for Miss Amelia before she died. I guess Miss Amelia took the girl to raise as her own."

Margie was a tad drunk. "How sad for the young girl."

David continued to answer her first question. "Bunker works for Miss Amelia. He keeps the girls safe and makes sure none of the customers get out of hand."

Margie, as usual, did not understand. "Why would they need his protection?"

"Well, sometimes the customer has too much to drink and shows his butt or he wants more and can't pay for it. That's when Bunker steps in. They seldom have any trouble, but if it comes, Bunker's the right man to have on your side."

Margie was trying to think with her head in a margarita fog. Moonlight Charlie's time at the bar was over. The paying customers were waiting for more of his magic. He moved away from the bar.

"Gotta go back to work. Gotta pay the rent. It was nice seeing you again. I hope you stick around. You a good swimmer?"

Moonlight Charlie was already in the middle of the room before Margie could register and answer his last and strange question. Margie talked out loud and quietly questioned herself. "Another musician? What's going on with me?"

Her thoughts were short lived when Moonlight Charlie started playing again and Ruby left her table to dance alone near the small stage. The crowd clapped again and made wild noises as she began to dance.

Ellie walked through the front door of Miss Amelia's house, followed by Bunker. The young men still waiting in the front room saw them both. Ellie looked into the room and spoke to Marli.

"Bunker's here, now. You need me for anything?"

Marli shook her head. "I'm fine. Everything's movin' right along. Bunker nodded to Marli and sat down in a chair near the front door. Ellie disappeared down the hallway and went into her bedroom located right next to Miss Amelia's room. When Ellie sat on her bed she could hear noises of pleasure coming from Miss Amelia's room.

The young man who paid two hundred dollars for one half hour with Miss Amelia was a Mayport sailor named Buster Freeman. Miss Amelia was far too much woman for him, but he was doing his best. After she sucked out all his juices in the first ten minutes, Miss Amelia directed Mr. Freeman down the path of sucking out her juices. It was as if he was there to please her. Even though he had paid for her services, it was most obvious Miss Amelia was in charge. She had his head between her big legs, as she rubbed her pelvic area back and forth to cause friction with her tender skin and his face. She even told him one time, "Just kiss me there like you were kissing my other lips. Don't be afraid to French kiss me there either." Miss Amelia moaned and moved her hips as Mr. Freeman lifted his head for a breath of air every now and then. It was a first for Mr. Freeman, but once he saw, felt and heard Miss Amelia's reaction to his penetrating tongue, he knew he would use his new found talent on the other women who chose to share a bed with him. Miss Amelia knew he would be a much better lover for the next woman he encountered.

Miss Amelia pulled Buster's head up and turned her body so they were both staring at each other's private areas. She pushed the back of his head until his face touched her again and wrapped her legs around him with her big thighs covering his ears. When Mr. Freeman felt her hot mouth on his manhood he pushed his tongue as deep as he could inside her, making Miss Amelia quiver and moan with pure delight. When the half hour was over Mr. Freeman would have paid again if he had the money.

Ruby had danced through three songs. All eyes, male and female watched her. Margie had never seen such enticing body movements. Ruby seemed to be directing all her sexual energy toward Moonlight Charlie. It was most obvious she wanted him. Ruby sat back down at her table with her two friends. Margie had not thought about Bunker during Ruby's dances. She addressed the new bartender as he worked behind the bar. "Where did that young girl take Bunker?"

The bartender lifted his head from his work. "He works at Miss Amelia's place on the busy weekends. Keeps things in order when them crazy young white boys don't respect the young ladies."

Margie squinted her eyes. "What ladies?"

He smiled. "The American Beach ladies of the evening." He turned to wait on other customers.

Ellie was young and protected but she knew how pretty she was when she looked in the mirror. The way men and women responded to her also reinforced her ego. Ellie was physically protected from the men who passed through Miss Amelia's door, but there was no way to protect her from the mental maturity she had developed from living in that "cat house". Her constant contact with so many women of low moral fiber had to skew her way of thinking. Ellie had seen naked men, naked women, sexual encounters and heard every sexual noise known to man. Even with Miss Amelia's protection, Ellie's sexual knowledge and understanding was far too extensive for a seventeen year old.

She was excited at the thought of becoming sexually active with a partner. Ellie had already learned about self gratification by watching through a key hole as one of Miss Amelia's girls masturbated for a customer. Ellie was twelve years old at the time and had been using the same technique ever since. She wanted to be with a man, see him naked, see his reaction to her perfect body and feel him inside her. Her mind was set. It was only a matter of opportunity and time. Ellie had fantasies of being with Moonlight Charlie.

Margie finished her third free margarita. It was the one that broke the camel's back. She was drunk as Cooter Brown. The bartender stepped up to her.

"You alright, ma'am?"

Margie smiled a goofy grin. "Not really. I can't feel my legs. I don't think I can stand up."

He smiled. "That Jose Cuervo has a tendency to do that to folks."

Moonlight Charlie stepped up behind her and put his hands on her shoulders. "That was my last song, Margie. I was hoping you might like to take a midnight swim with Moonlight Charlie, but why don't you just let David Lott take you back to Miss Amelia's and get you settled for the night. Perhaps we'll have another opportunity in the future." David Lott was a good man. He was too cool.

Ruby was standing nearby and heard Moonlight Charlie's conversation with the new girl, Margie. She watched him assist

Margie to the front door of the lounge. Ruby had been hoping for a swim or body tumble with him, but she realized she would have to wait her turn. She was disappointed but she knew if she wanted a man she could have another.

As Moonlight Charlie assisted Margie to the front door she looked back toward Ruby with a silly smile on her face. In only a second Ruby realized why she thought she had seen the new girl somewhere before. She recognized Margie as a Mayport girl and one of the sisters who worked at the general store. She wondered what a white Mayport girl was doing in the Honey Dripper Lounge, getting drunk, leaving with Moonlight Charlie and staying at Miss Amelia's whorehouse. Ruby usually minded her own business, but she wanted answers to her questions.

David Lott opened the front door to Miss Amelia's house and supported Margie at the same time. She could walk, but needed him so she would not stagger and lose her balance. Miss Amelia was escorting four young sailors to the door. They were out of time and money. Buster Freeman was one of the four standing at the door. Miss Amelia patted him on the butt.

"You made my night, Buster. I hope we get to see you again."

Buster nodded his head as Miss Amelia turned her attention to David as he maneuvered Margie through the door and past the sailors.

"What ya got there, Moonlight?"

David smiled. "I think it's one of your new tenants."

Miss Amelia looked closer. "Well, I'll be damned. It's Margie. You are somethin' else, boy." She closed the door. "Where'd ya find this pretty thing?" She continued before he could answer. "No, don't tell me. The Honey Dripper strikes again."

"Yes ma'am. She just landed in my lap and here we are."

"That seems to happen to you quite often, don't it?"

Miss Amelia turned to see Ellie standing at the foot of

the stairs. "Ellie, go upstairs and open sixteen with my key." Miss Amelia handed Ellie her "goodie key" that opened all the doors. A woman with such an active boarding house had to be able to enter any room at any time. The young beauty looked at David, smiled and then ran up the stairs to the second floor to do as Miss Amelia had instructed.

David supported Margie up the stairs and Ellie was standing at the opened bedroom door when David arrived with his new intoxicated friend. He moved her past Ellie and walked her to the bed. As he eased Margie onto the bed, she pulled him down on top of her and kissed him passionately. The tequila had taken away what little inhibitions Margie had.

Ellie's beautiful eyes lit up. She was not jealous. She was envious. She was way ahead of her time. David was surprised when Ellie closed the door, leaving him alone with the easy and more than willing Margie. She returned to her room to get lost in her own fantasy world.

Once Moonlight Charlie was alone with Margie and she was more than willing to please him, he did not pass up the opportunity to be with the beautiful newcomer. Not many men would walk away from such a moment.

Margie was the aggressor as they both removed their clothes. It was as if she could not wait to unleash her sexual talents on the music man. Her state of intoxication only added to her sexual drive but she still wanted him without the influence of the tequila. She was wild and primitive. Moonlight Charlie let her take over and have her way with him. He liked the way Margie seemed to melt her body unto his. When she pushed her bare breasts to his bare chest it was as if they melted together. Margie did not know it, but she shared that sexual trait with her little sister, Sofia. It was a great feeling for any man fortunate enough to be with either one of the sisters.

When he reached down and touched her, hot body fluids covered his fingers and palm of his hand; another great feeling for him. Margie surprised David when she turned away, positioned herself on her hands and knees, and offered her perfect backside to him. It was her favorite position. David did not hesitate. He knew what to do as he positioned himself behind her. Margie was so wet that he went deep into her with his first push. She moaned with delight and had her usual instructions for David.

"Do it hard. As hard as you can."

Miss Amelia's house was an interesting structure. It was actually built to be what it was; a house of ill repute. The house had secret exits and entrances, so the customers could sneak in or out if they had to. Spaces between the walls allowed movement and hiding places. Miss Amelia used these areas from time to time to watch the activity of the girls and for their protection in case a customer got out of hand. If she did watch through the walls, it was strictly for business and not for pleasure. Miss Amelia did not use the areas very often, but Ellie used them almost on a daily basis.

Ellie had seen so many sexual activities at her young age that it could only have warped her young mind. She touched herself as she watched Moonlight Charlie slamming his body against Margie's. It was good for all three of them.

Margie woke up alone in the rented bed. Her new friend was not there with her. She could feel the uncomfortable effects of the hard liquor, but liked the feeling she had about her late night sexual activity. She did not feel violated as she had before. Margie had been a willing participant.

Margie was still a woman on the run and with her latest act of revenge in Vilano Beach near St. Augustine she knew staying on the move was probably her only choice. She was still naked as she sat up on the edge of the bed and placed her feet on the hardwood floor. She shook her head when she realized her butt was sore. There was a knock at the door. She thought of Moonlight Charlie as she pulled the bed sheet around her body.

"Yes, who is it?"

"It's Miss Amelia, Margie. May I come in?"

"Yes, ma'am. I don't think it's locked."

Miss Amelia opened the door and entered the room. Margie remained on the bed. "I'm sorry to bother you, but you really slept late. Checkout's in an hour. I just wanted you to know that."

Margie had no idea she had slept so late. "Oh, I'm sorry. I didn't mean to sleep this late."

"That's fine suga'. No harm done. You feelin' alright?"

"Yes, I'm fine."

Miss Amelia smiled. "I'd try to talk you into stayin' another day, but ya seem so hell bent on movin' on. I didn't want to interfere with your plans. I know when a person' on the move."

Margie looked at Miss Amelia. "What makes you say that?"

"Just a feelin'. I've seen enough folks on the run in my time. I'm usually right, but I could be wrong."

Margie pulled the sheet up covering even more of her naked body. Miss Amelia had more to say. "It ain't none of my business, but this is a good place to get your thoughts together. A beautiful woman like you could make a place for herself right here. She could become a new person. It's happened before and will happen again. Why can't it be 'My Little Margie'? I'd like to discuss a business deal with you. Something I think will benefit both of us." Miss Amelia walked to the door. "Let me know if you're interested. If not, it was great having you here and good luck."

Miss Amelia left the room but did not close the door. Margie stood up, holding he sheet to her naked body and walked to close the door. As she touched the door, Ellie passed in the hall. Their eyes met. Margie smiled.

"Good morning. It's Ellie, right?"

Ellie nodded and walked on down the hall. Margie shrugged her shoulders and as she pushed the door she saw the door to Moonlight Charlie's room open. Her heart raced in anticipation of seeing her new lover. Margie was disappointed when one of the cleaning maids came from the room. She was preparing the room for the next paying customer. David Lott was gone.

Mary C. was sitting at the bar in Smitty's Lounge on First Street in Jacksonville Beach, Florida. The lounge was located near the Board Walk and a popular watering hole for the locals and the sailors from the Mayport Naval Base. The pool tables were always filled and the cracking of the "ball breaks" was a common sound during the evening. Mary C. was planning to have one drink, perhaps shoot a game or two of pool and then head back to Mayport. She was on her own but not really looking for a male encounter. Her thoughts were on Jason and her grandson, Billy. She was glad they were home with her. Mary C. had decided to have one double Jack Daniels and coke and then go to the Red Barn Bar-B-Q for a take-out for her and Mr. King. She would surprise Mr. King with a late night jumbo pork sandwich and a bag of onion rings. She smiled at the thought of him being up all night with heart burn, but she knew he would eat it all and worry about the consequences later.

Smitty's was filling up with young sailors and a few locals. As usual, Mary C. looked sexy and confident. All eyes were on her at one time or another. She looked into the large mirror hanging on the wall behind the bar and could see the young handsome sailors as they moved around the pool tables. It was obvious most of them were close to Jason's age and she was old enough to be their mother.

A group of the men had been watching her and they were placing bets as to which one she would talk to and allow them to buy her a drink. There were ten other women in the room sitting at tables or at the bar. The men out numbered the women three to one. Mary C. seemed to be one of the women without a male companion. One sailor bet fifty dollars that he could talk to her, and buy her a drink. Four of his friends had taken the bet and he was in a position to win or lose two hundred dollars.

The young man was nervous as he left his friends and walked toward the beautiful lady at the bar. He had a great deal riding on his ability to be charming. Mary C. watched him in the mirror but did not turn around as he walked up behind her. He sat down on the bar stool next to her and ordered a beer from the bartender. Mary C. continued to watch him in the mirror but did not turn to him. He stared at her, hoping she would turn his way. She did not. He looked back at his smiling friends and took a deep breath.

"I'm Buster. Would you allow me to buy you a drink?"

Mary C. did not turn his way. She continued to watch him in the mirror. Mary C. knew things.

"Well now, Buster, what's the bet?"

Buster's face went beet red. "Excuse me?"

"The Bet! What's the bet? How much money's on the line for you if I let you buy me a drink and sit here with me? Do you make more if I kiss ya or if we leave together? I need to know what I'm up against here and just how important I am to you at this very moment."

Buster's throat went dry and he had no charming words. Mary C. would see his frustration. She turned to him and smiled and kissed him on his lips.

"I'll have a Jack and coke and you can sit with me after you go collect your money." Mary C was too cool for the world she was locked into. Buster walked to where his friends were still standing and took his winnings.

After his short but profitable meeting with his shocked friends, Buster went back to the bar to sit with Mary C. He did not return to play pool with his financially limited friends. He could always be with them, but he knew opportunities with a woman like Mary C. would not come very many times in his life. He was hoping for much more.

They talked for about half an hour. Buster did most of the talking. He talked about not wanting to go back to sea and how he hated being away from his home and family in Tampa. He had a girlfriend he wanted to marry. Her father was a Baptist minister and kept a tight hold on his beautiful daughter. The old saying about the preacher's daughter being wild and free did not pertain to his true love. Mary C. never talked about herself so she listened to the excited young man. Buster found a moment of courage.

"Is there a chance I could be naked with you? I have a room at the Sand Piper Hotel if you would like to go there with me."

Mary C. never changed her expression. "Seems like you are quite prepared for a well planned evening."

"Yes, you're right. But, I didn't think I'd meet someone like you."

There was a back entrance to the Sand Piper Hotel on the Board Walk side. Buster's room was near that back door on the first floor. He had rented that same room a number of times so he had a place to stay if he got too drunk to go back to the Naval Base or he got lucky with one of the local young ladies. No one saw the two of them come through the back door and enter the room.

As soon as they walked in, Mary C. began undressing. Buster was surprised but pleased when she stood naked in front of him. Her body was hard and youthful. Her stomach was flat and her butt was round and tight. He undressed as she walked past him.

"Come take a shower with me and we'll get to know each other."

Mary C. was an expert at taking a shower before the sexual encounter. Buster's heart raced when she pushed her wet body against his and his hard chest touched her hard breasts. His erection was quick and substantial. She reached down and held him in one hand and lathered him with soap with the other hand. When the water rinsed off the white lather, Mary C. handed him the bar of soap.

"Now, you do me." She turned her back to him, put both hands on the shower wall and presented her perfect buttocks to him.

Buster did not hesitate to rub the bar of soap over her butt cheeks until they were both covered with the white lather. His hands slid freely across her tight skin. He pushed his soap covered thumb inside her. It went deep because of the sudsy lubricant. Mary C. moaned with the quick and surprising anal stimulation. She even pushed her butt toward his hand to make his thumb go deeper. Buster removed his thumb, but quickly replaced it with another finger, causing a deeper penetration. Mary C. squirmed and moaned again, but did not move away from his hand. As she continued to push against his hand, Buster was able to reach between her legs with the same hand and strategically place two fingers inside her womanhood at the same time his thumb was also deep inside her.

Mary C.'s movements and noises excited Buster to the extent he knew he was going to explode and release his juices onto the tile shower floor.

"I'm too excited. I don't think I can hold it."

Mary C. turned away from the wall, breaking the vaginal and anal contact with his fingers. She squatted down on the shower floor and took his blood filled member in her hand guiding it to her mouth. The early stimulation and the heat from her lips caused an instant explosion Buster could not control. He just let it go. He had no choice.

Buster looked down as the water from the shower bounced off of Mary C.'s back. Her lips remained locked onto him until all his sexual juices left his body. He had to get her into the bed.

There was no way Buster Freeman was prepared for a woman like Mary C., but he had learned a great sexual lesson from his encounter with Miss Amelia and how to satisfy his sexual partner with oral stimulation as an intense prelude to the sexual relations to come. His foreplay was second to none and he hoped it would be his sexual trademark. Besides, Buster liked making the woman squirm and the feel and taste of her fluids on his tongue.

Buster kissed Mary C. once and moved his head down her body. His head moved between her breasts and she loved feeling his tongue touching her. She felt his tongue continue down her stomach, into her naval, stopping above her pelvic hair line. When his downward plunge ended his head was between her legs. It was easy for Mary C. to relax and assist him as he pushed her legs wide open and placed his mouth in the perfect place. His wet tongue and the heat from her skin sent Mary C.'s blood flow in abnormal directions, making her light-headed in a matter of seconds.

Her previous lovers were more interested in their pleasure than hers. She liked the fact this young man was going to settle in for as long as she could withstand his flickering tongue, lips and even biting teeth. Mary C. closed her eyes, opened her legs even wider and allowed the young sailor to have his way with her.

Buster Freeman buried his face between Mary C.'s legs with his tongue and lips wreaking havoc on her womanhood. She had no watch to check but she estimated in her head that Buster had been eating her for at least a full ten minutes. It was a first for Mary C. It would have been a first for many women. She could feel her stomach muscles contracting and actually thought her body fluids were coming up from her toes. Mary C. knew her release and explosion was going to be one of Biblical proportion and she was not prepared. She wanted to be able to handle the young man and be the dominant force, but Buster had sexually moved her to a new and uncharted place. No one had ever taken such time to be sure she was satisfied first.

Mary C. had not had the pleasure of a man's head between her legs in quite some time. She had always been a true fan and willing participant in the area of oral stimulation, but the release of her body fluids was always far too intense and moved her into a different sexual dimension and state of pure pleasure. Usually, when she exploded, Mary C. would slam her legs together, squeezing her sexual partner with her thighs. Then in the same motion she would roll to one side in order to break the contact with her pleaser. Her muscular legs and adrenalin flow would give her the strength to move the man anywhere she wanted in order for her to free herself.

Mary C. knew she was going to have the most intense climax to ever take over her body and senses. She thought for only a second about how she would repay this young man for such a superior level of satisfaction. She smiled at what she would do once he had completed his wonderful assault.

Mary C. decided she would allow him the ultimate sexual privilege. She knew the majority of men wanted to perform anal intercourse with their partners, but the permission to do so was very limited. She would reward him for his outstanding sexual effort and ask him to penetrate her anally. It was the least she could do.

It was time. It was Biblical. The Old Testament sexual explosion was at hand. Mary C. tried to pull away from his hold, but Buster cupped her butt cheeks with his strong hands and held her in position as he drove his tongue deeper. Her stomach contractions caused her legs to cramp as he held her against his face. It was not normal for her to release the amount of sexual fluid she felt flowing to Buster's face. She had never felt so helpless and out of control. It had to end.

As the hot liquid touched his face, Buster felt Mary C.'s body quiver. He held her in place. Mary C. knew she was going to faint and gave one last push to free her body from her capturer. She slammed her legs together around his head, locking her feet and ankles in a scissor type hold. Mary C. twisted her body to the right, turning over completely onto her cramping stomach. Her movement broke his suction. Buster had felt such a leg squeeze before but he was not prepared for the strong and violent twisting of his head. It was like when a gator clamps down on its victim and then rolls over on its side to tear the flesh from the bone. Mary C. demonstrated her very own "gator roll". It was fast and strong. She did not hear Buster's pitiful gasp for air, but she did hear the awful cracking noise when his neck broke. She released her hold when she felt his limp body and dead weight. Mary C had no doubt the young man was dead in the bed. She sat up, took a deep breath and put her hand on his heart. It wasn't to feel for a heart beat, she already knew he was gone. Mary C. was an expert at death. It was just to say she was sorry and to thank him for the pleasure he had provided her.

Mary C. knew she would not report the unfortunate accident to the local authorities. She was calm, cool and collected as she got dressed and made sure she left no personal items in the room. In a matter of minutes she was walking out the back door onto the wooden slats of the Board Walk. It was only 10:30 so the Board Walk was still busy with the late night fun seekers. She moved into the crowd and made her way to her car. She stopped at the Red Barn for a take-out Bar-B-Q for her, Jason and John King. Her destination would be Mr. King's Haunted House in Mayport, Florida, U.S.A.